Originally published in French in 2018 as *Jack et le temps perdu*

First published in Canada, the U.S., and the U.K. by Greystone Books in 2020

20 21 22 23 24 5 4 3 2 1

Greystone Kids / Greystone Books Ltd.
greystonebooks.com

Cataloguing data available from Library and Archives Canada
ISBN 978-1-77164-757-1 (cloth)
ISBN 978-1-77164-758-8 (epub)

MIX
Paper from responsible sources
FSC® C016973

Copy editing by Dawn Loewen
Proofreading by DoEun Kwon
English jacket and text design by Sara Gillingham Studio
Jacket illustration by Delphie Côté-Lacroix
Printed and bound in China on ancient-forest-friendly paper by 1010 Printing International Ltd.

Greystone Books gratefully acknowledges the Musqueam, Squamish, and Tsleil-Waututh peoples on whose land our office is located.

Greystone Books thanks the Canada Council for the Arts, the British Columbia Arts Council, the Province of British Columbia through the Book Publishing Tax Credit, and the Government of Canada for supporting our publishing activities.

Canada
Canada Council for the Arts Conseil des arts du Canada
BRITISH COLUMBIA
BRITISH COLUMBIA ARTS COUNCIL
An agency of the Province of British Columbia

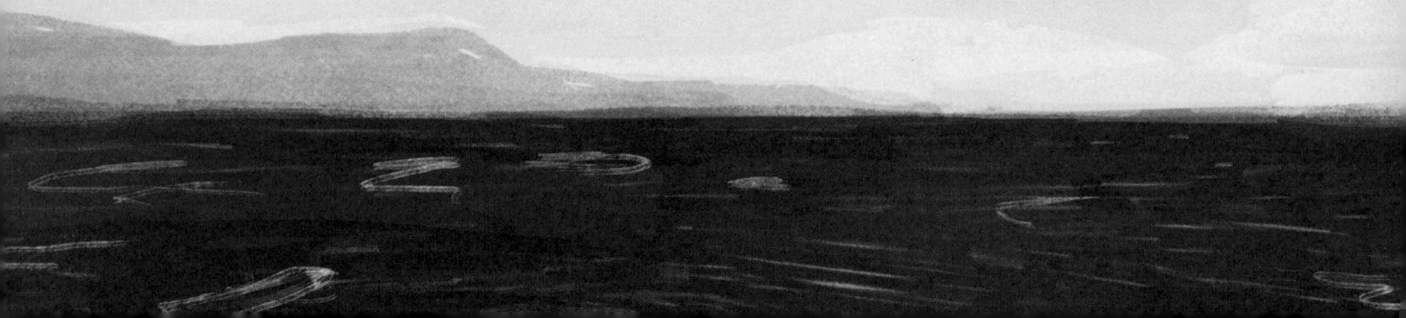

Stéphanie Lapointe & Delphie Côté-Lacroix

TRANSLATED BY Arielle Aaronson

HOW JACK LOST TIME

GREYSTONE KIDS

GREYSTONE BOOKS · VANCOUVER / BERKELEY

Sometimes I raise my eyes and look with sympathy at my brother the ocean: he feigns the infinite, but I know that he, too, everywhere comes up against his bounds, and hence all this fury, all this roar.

ROMAIN GARY, *PROMISE AT DAWN*
(TRANS. JOHN MARKHAM BEACH)

Human madness is oftentimes a cunning and most feline thing. When you think it fled, it may have but become transfigured into some still subtler form.

HERMAN MELVILLE, *MOBY DICK*

TO JULES,
MY INSPIRATION,
A STORY WITH A BIT OF ACTION.

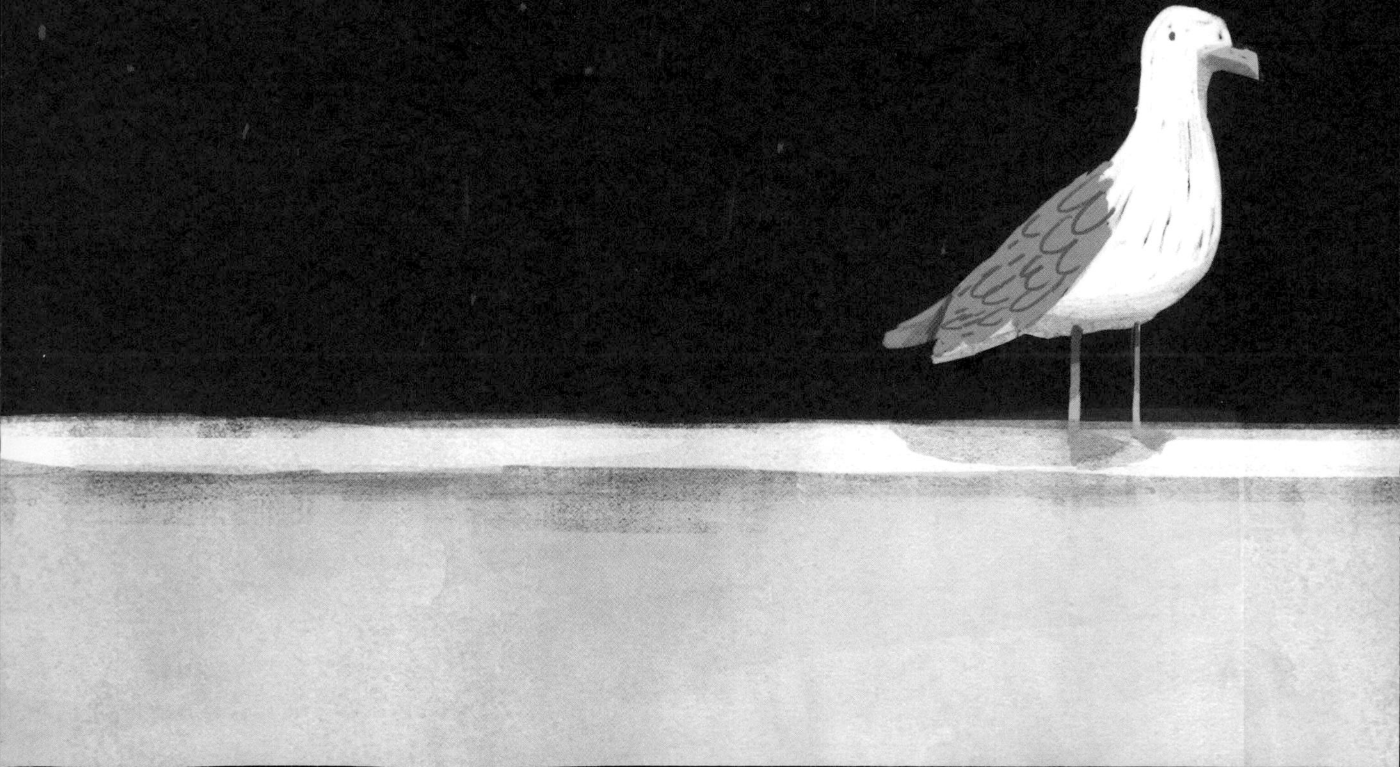

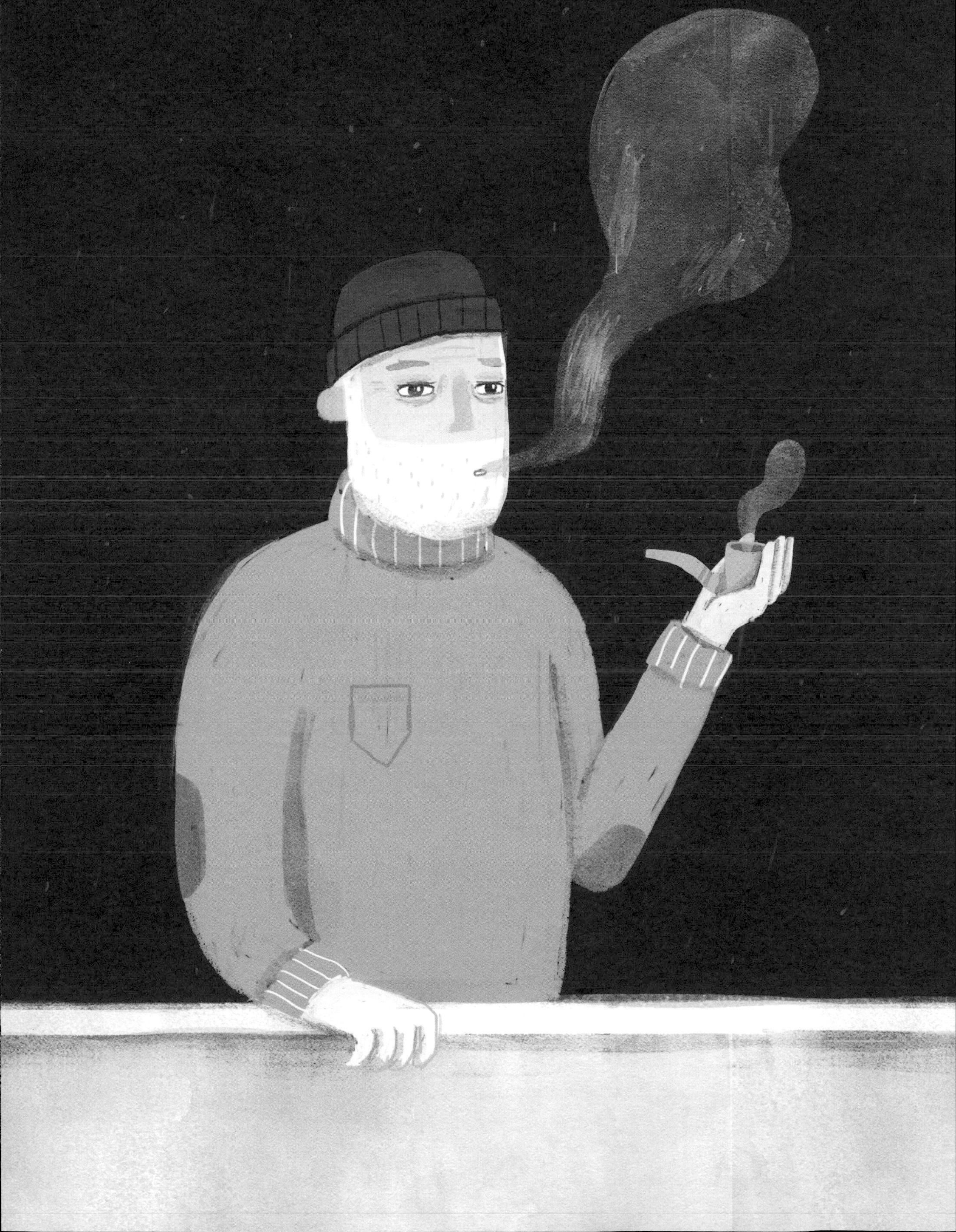

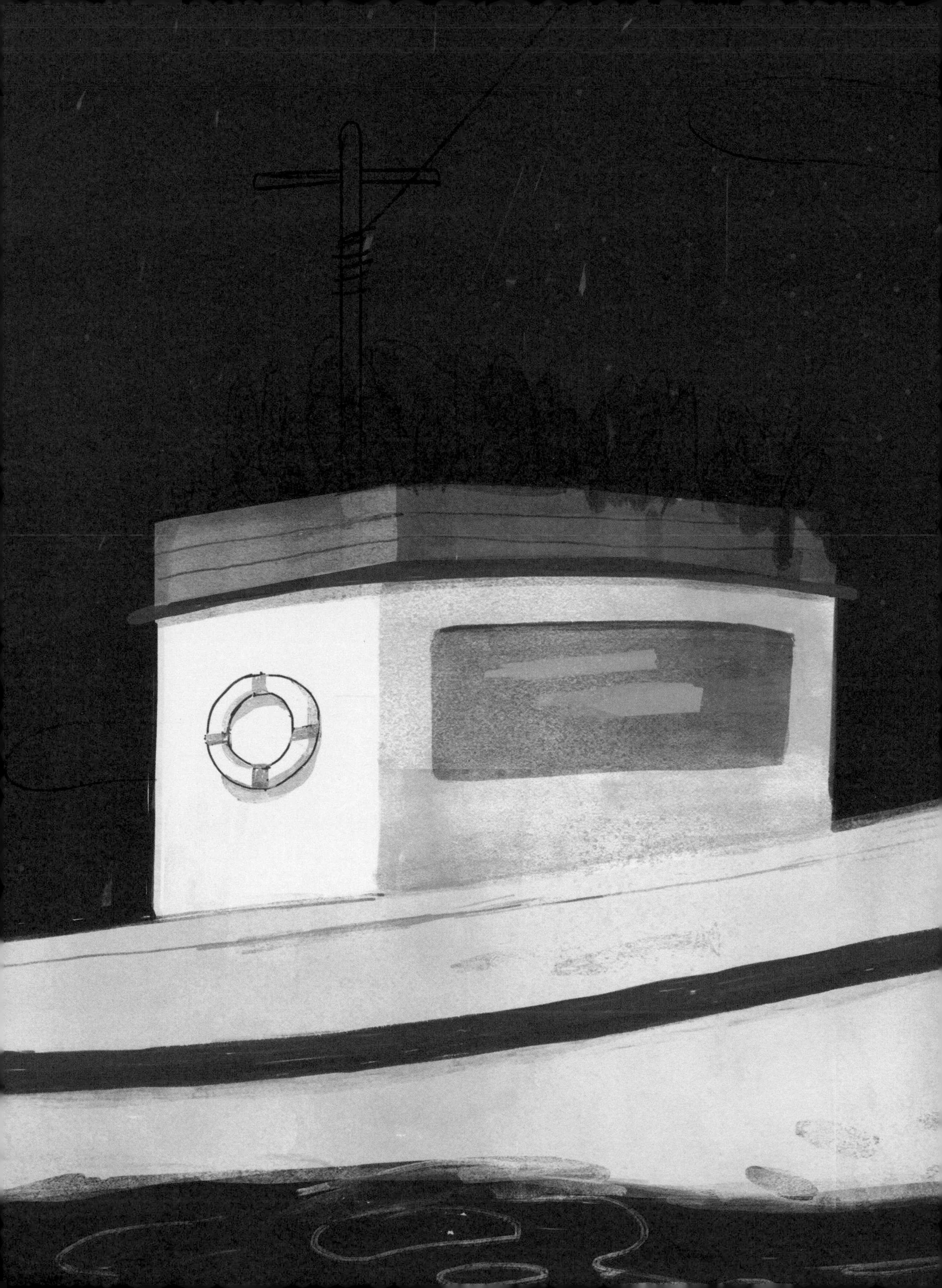

on his boat.

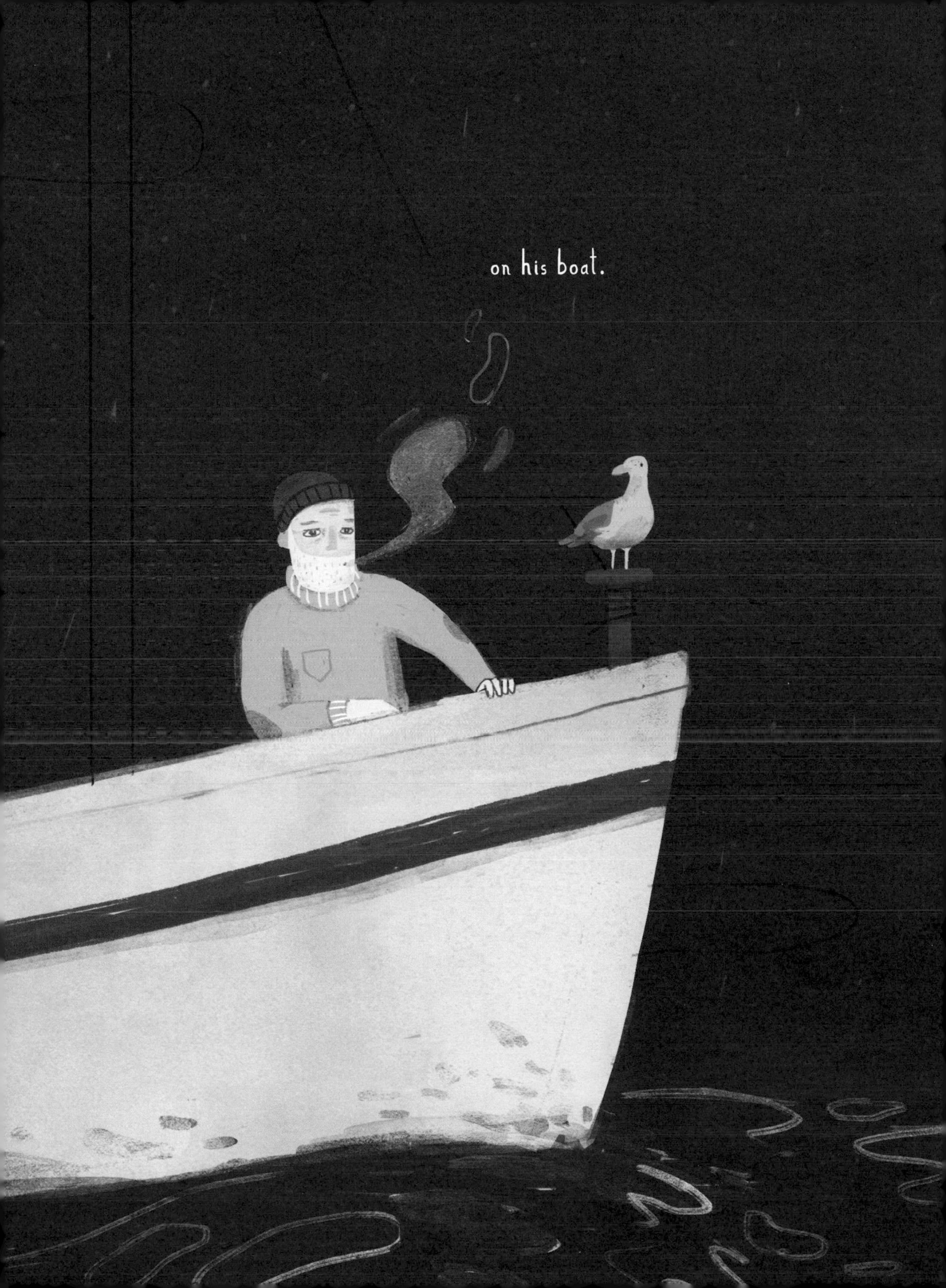

And to be absolutely
certain
he would never have to leave

his boat
(except in an emergency, of course),

Jack had even learned to garden.

Carrots,
turnips,
potatoes,
beets—

Jack knew how to grow everything
and grew everything
on his boat
(where the sun beat down).

No.
Jack never needed anything.

Except, perhaps,

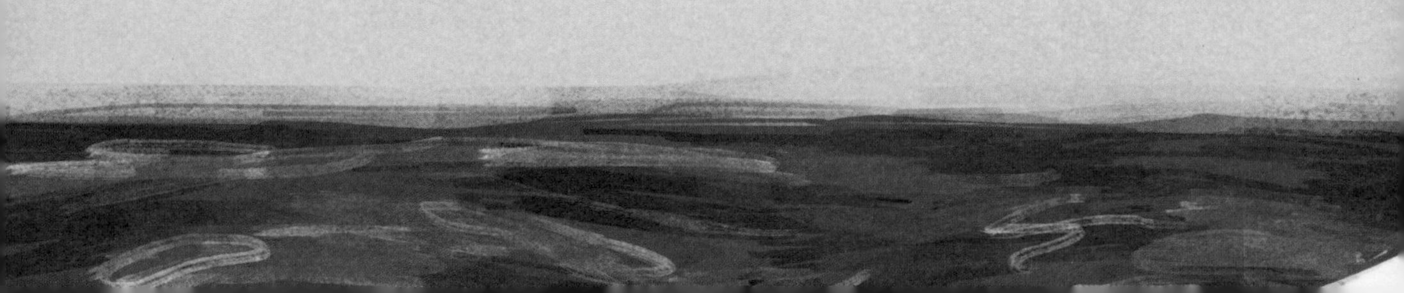

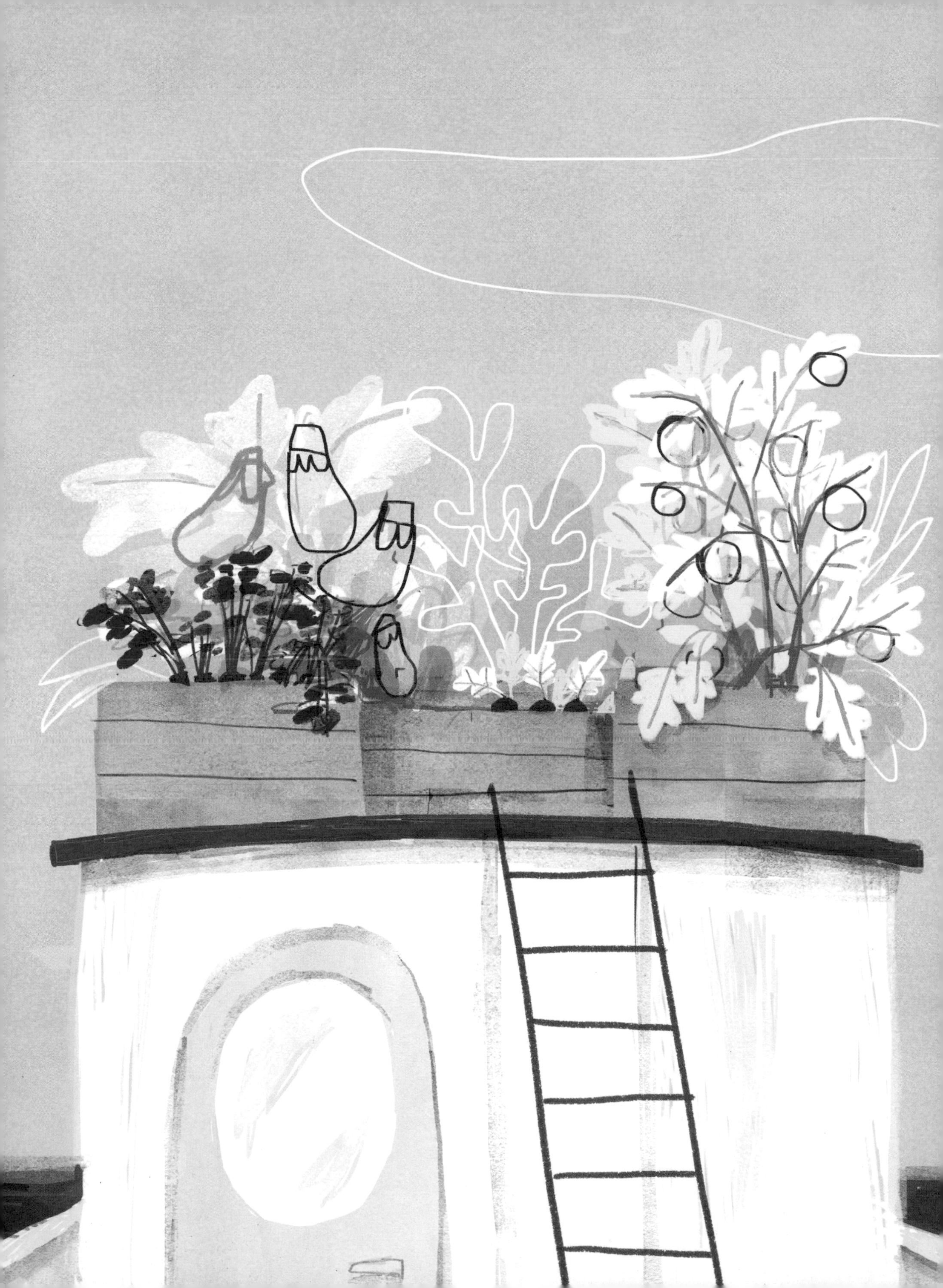

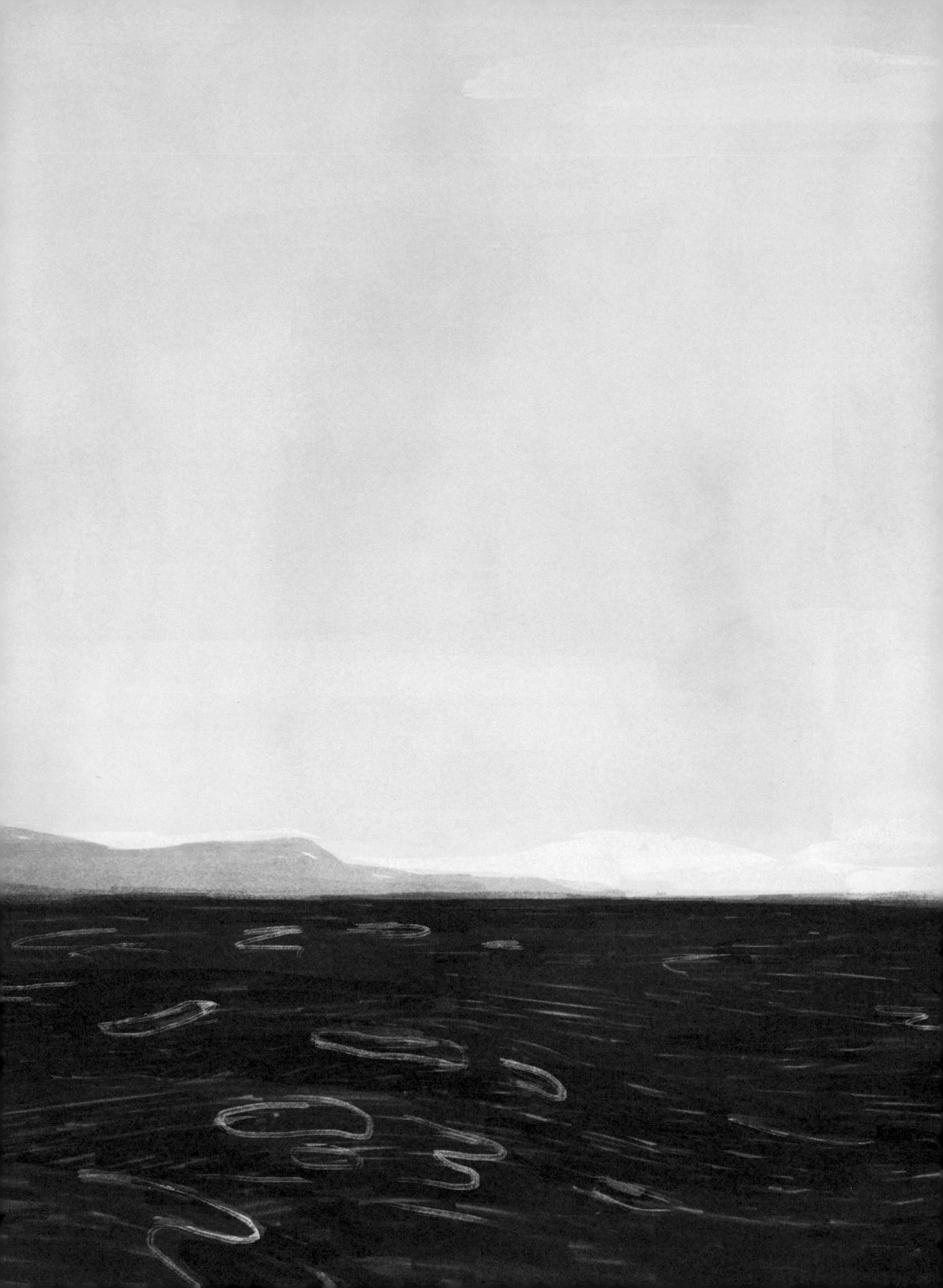

company.

When Jack felt lonely
(at night)
he smoked his pipe
and he read.

And since Jack often felt lonely
(at night)
he smoked his pipe
and he read

a lot.

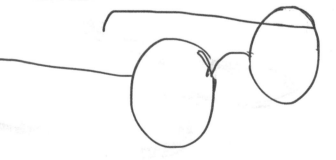

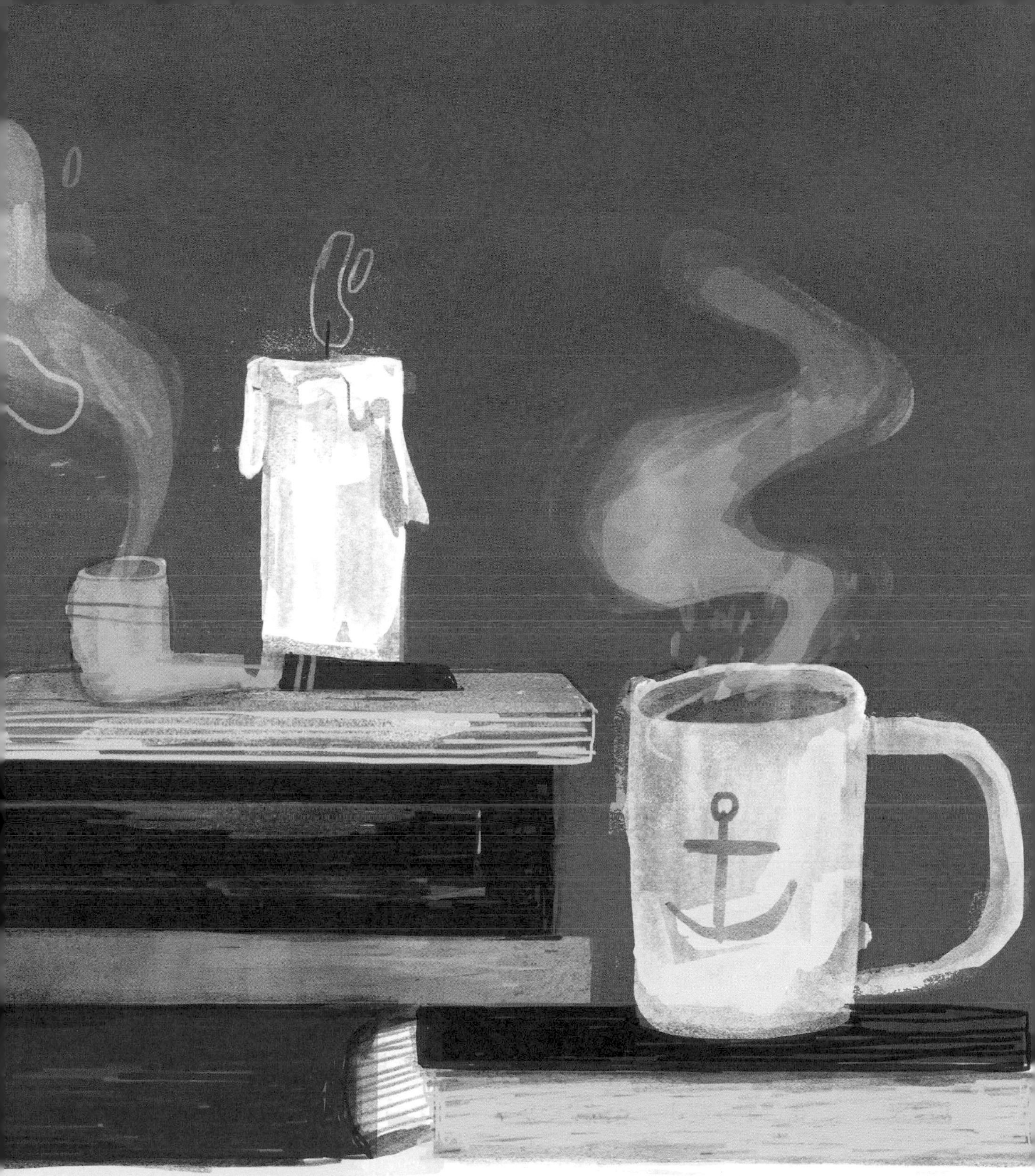

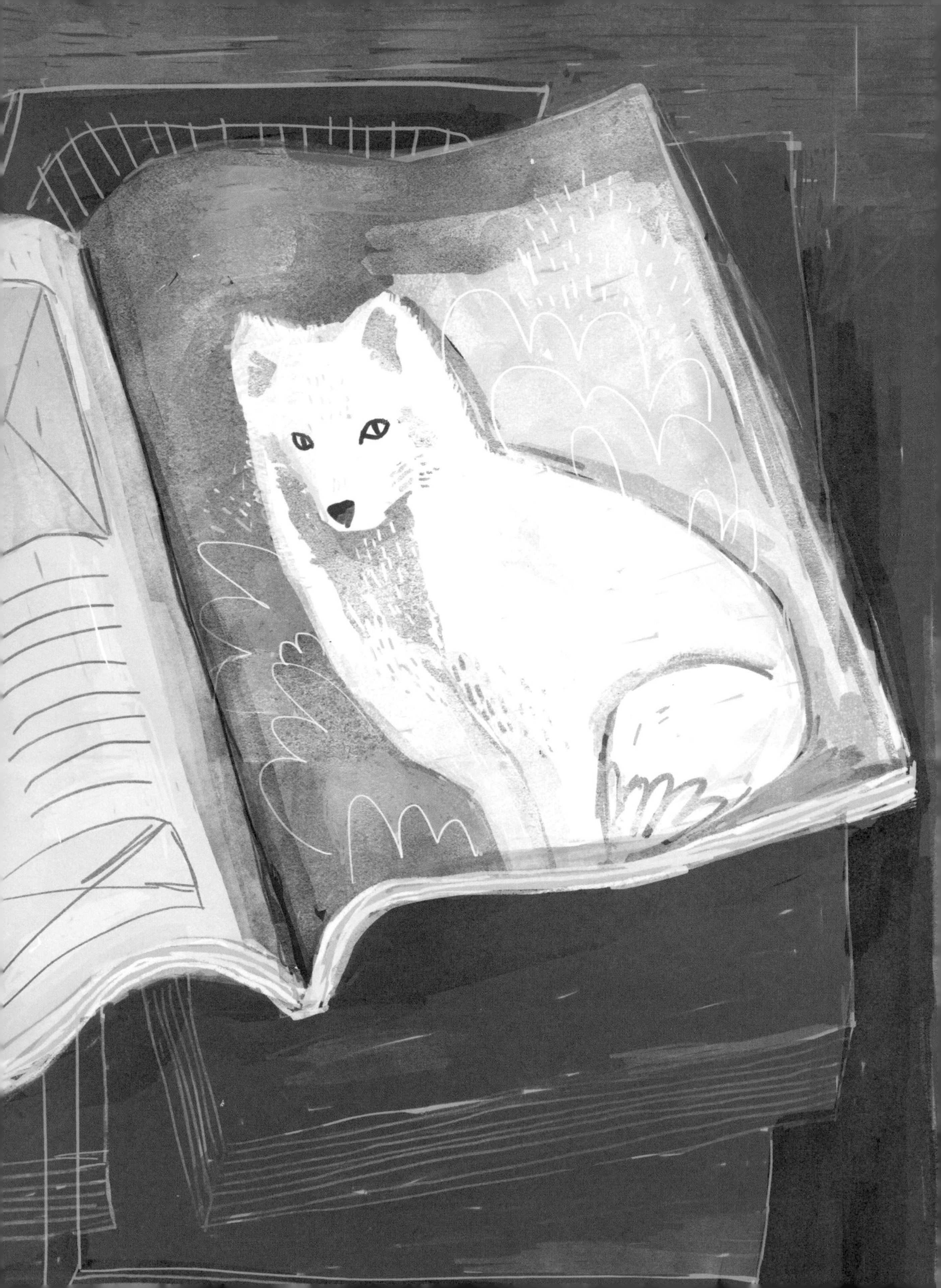

Jack read about
everything
and about

nothing.

Jack learned
that there were twelve kinds of foxes
in the world,
and not one more.

Once, he'd even told
the night air
that his favorite was

the arctic fox.

For some reason.

Jack had also read
an entire book explaining
everything there was to know
about building a real
wood cabin

and learned that in under two months,
with two strong men,
it could be done.

Once,
he'd even told
the night air
that he could build
his own wood cabin
by himself
in under six weeks.

For some reason.

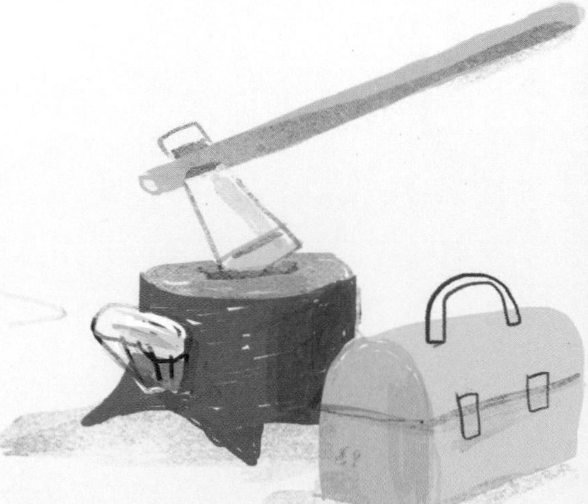

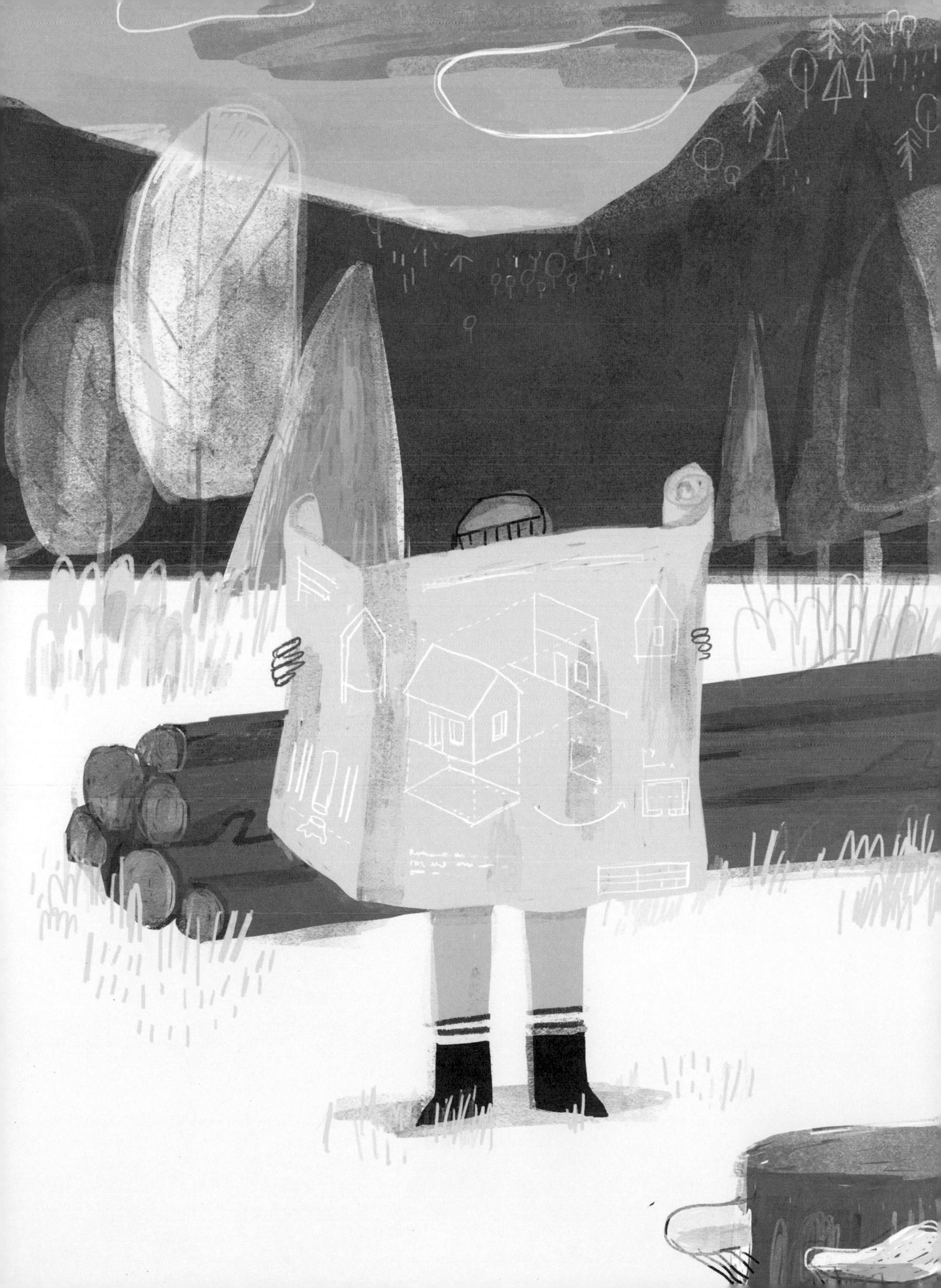

Nobody
knew what was in
Jack's heart.

So everybody drew the same
conclusions,

telling
anyone who would listen

that Jack simply
wasn't
a captain

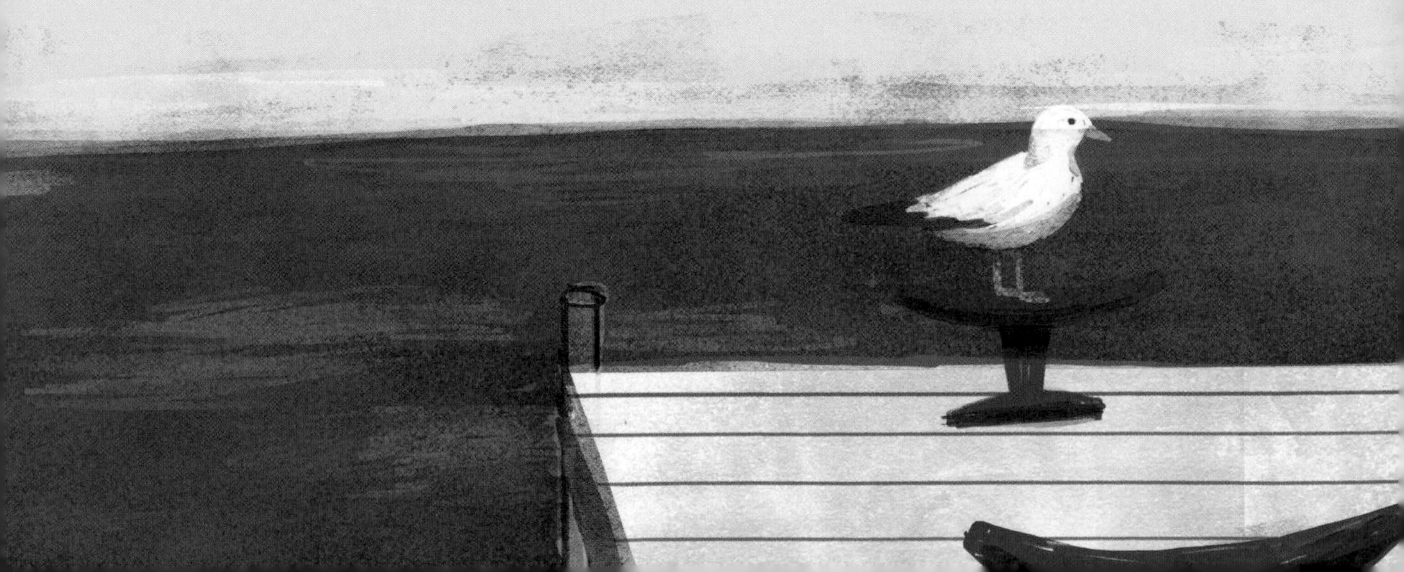

like the others.

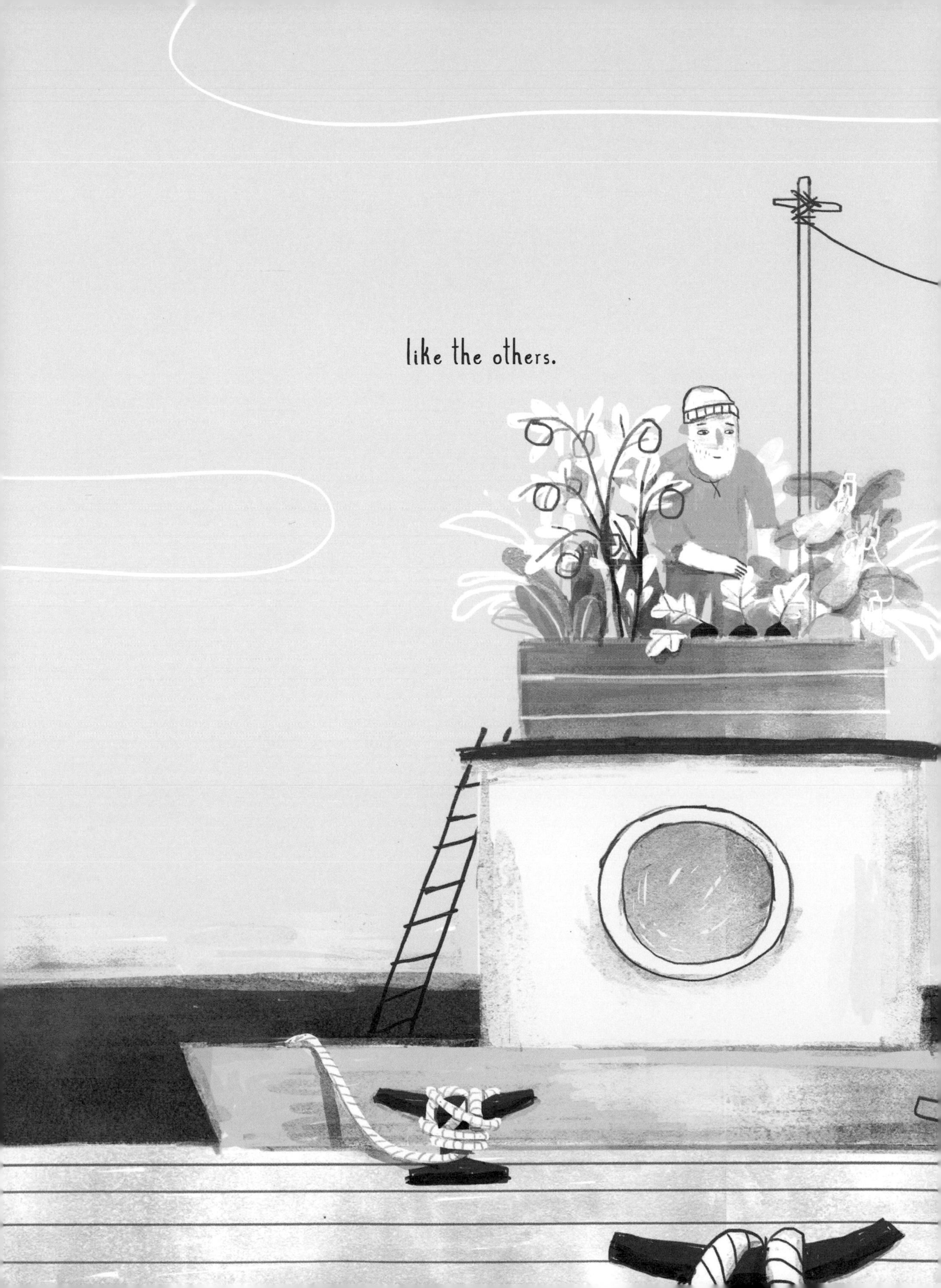

After all,
most captains
only care about

stretches of sky,
sunsets,
the latest anchors, and nets
of all sizes—

which left him completely indifferent.

He wasn't even interested
in fish,
of any kind.

So whenever one got caught
in his net
Jack threw it back
pronto.

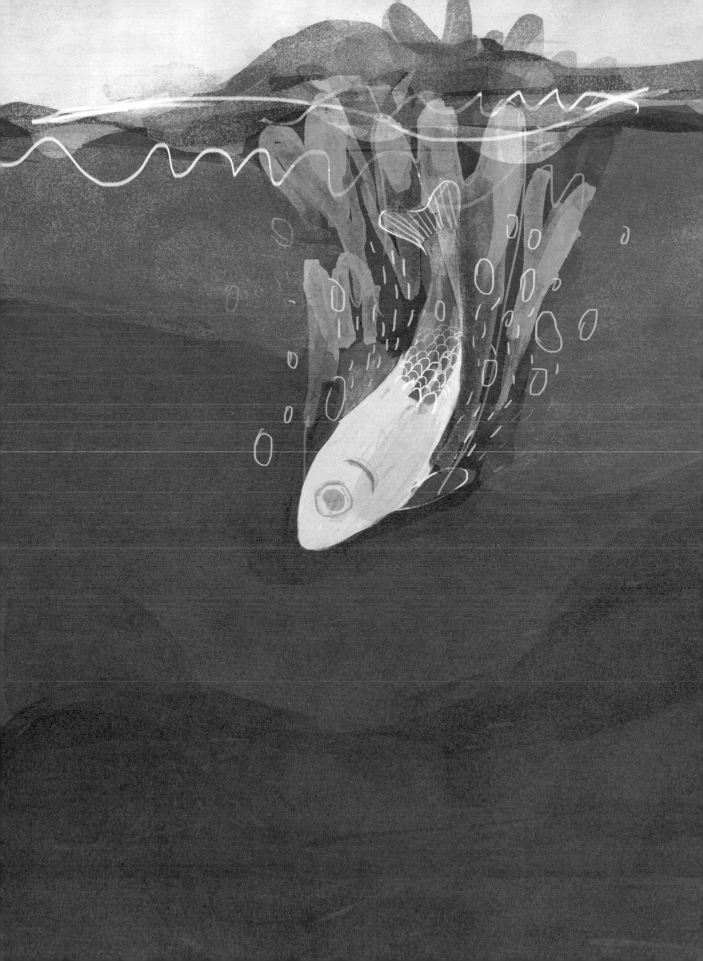

Scandalmongers
all said Jack was
crazy.

But the scandalmongers
were wrong.

Jack wasn't
crazy.

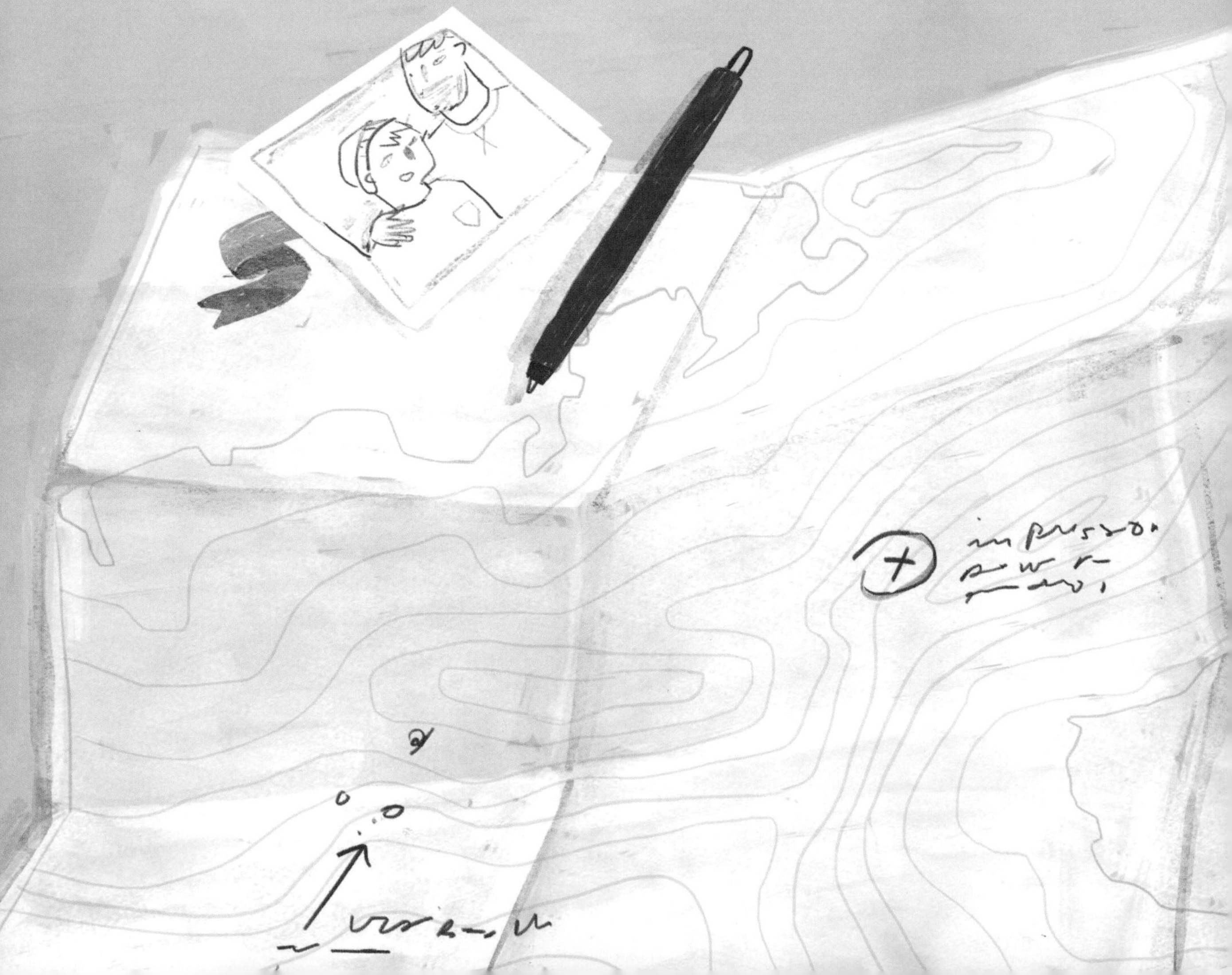

Let's just say he was consumed
with one
quest:

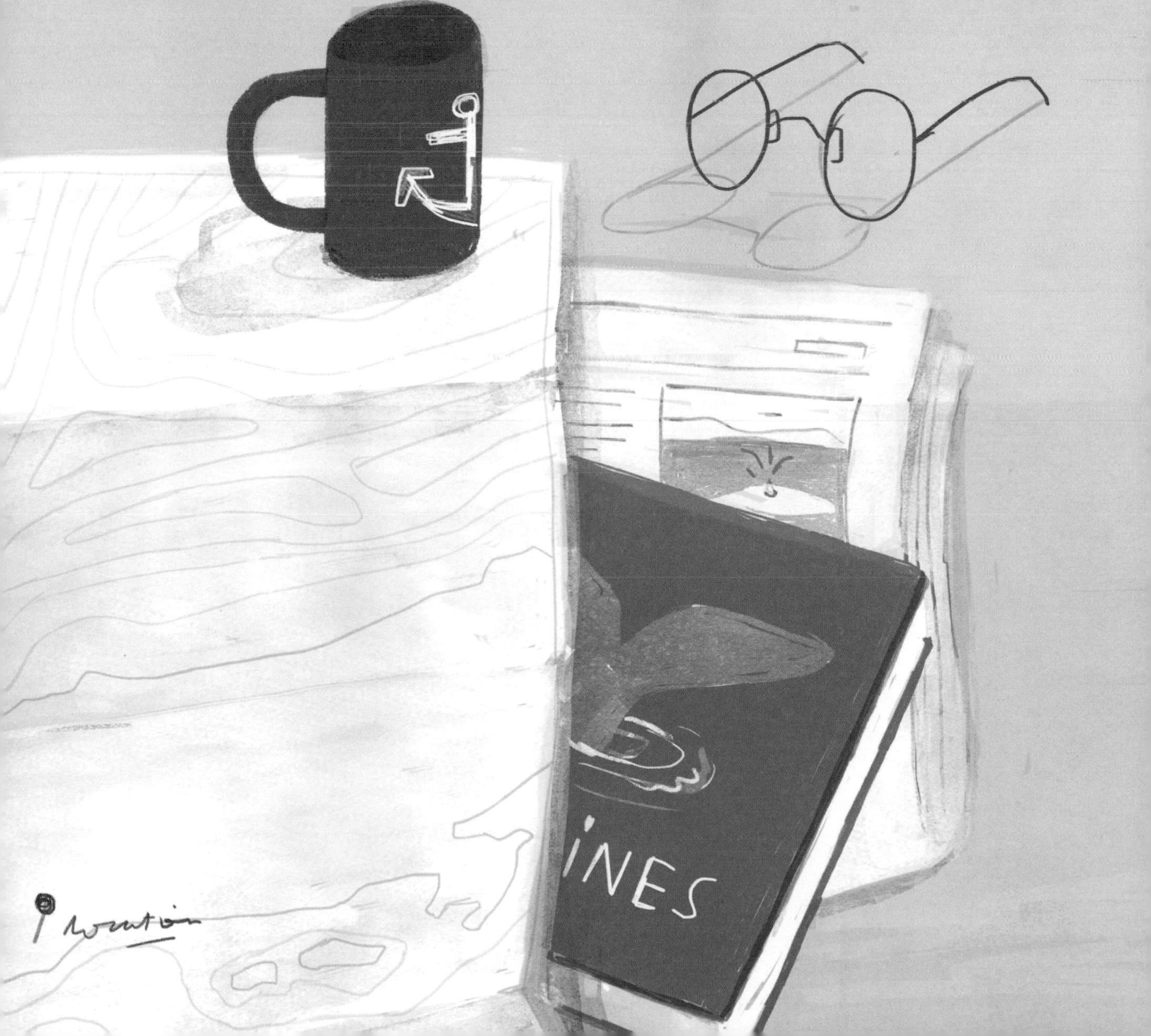
INES

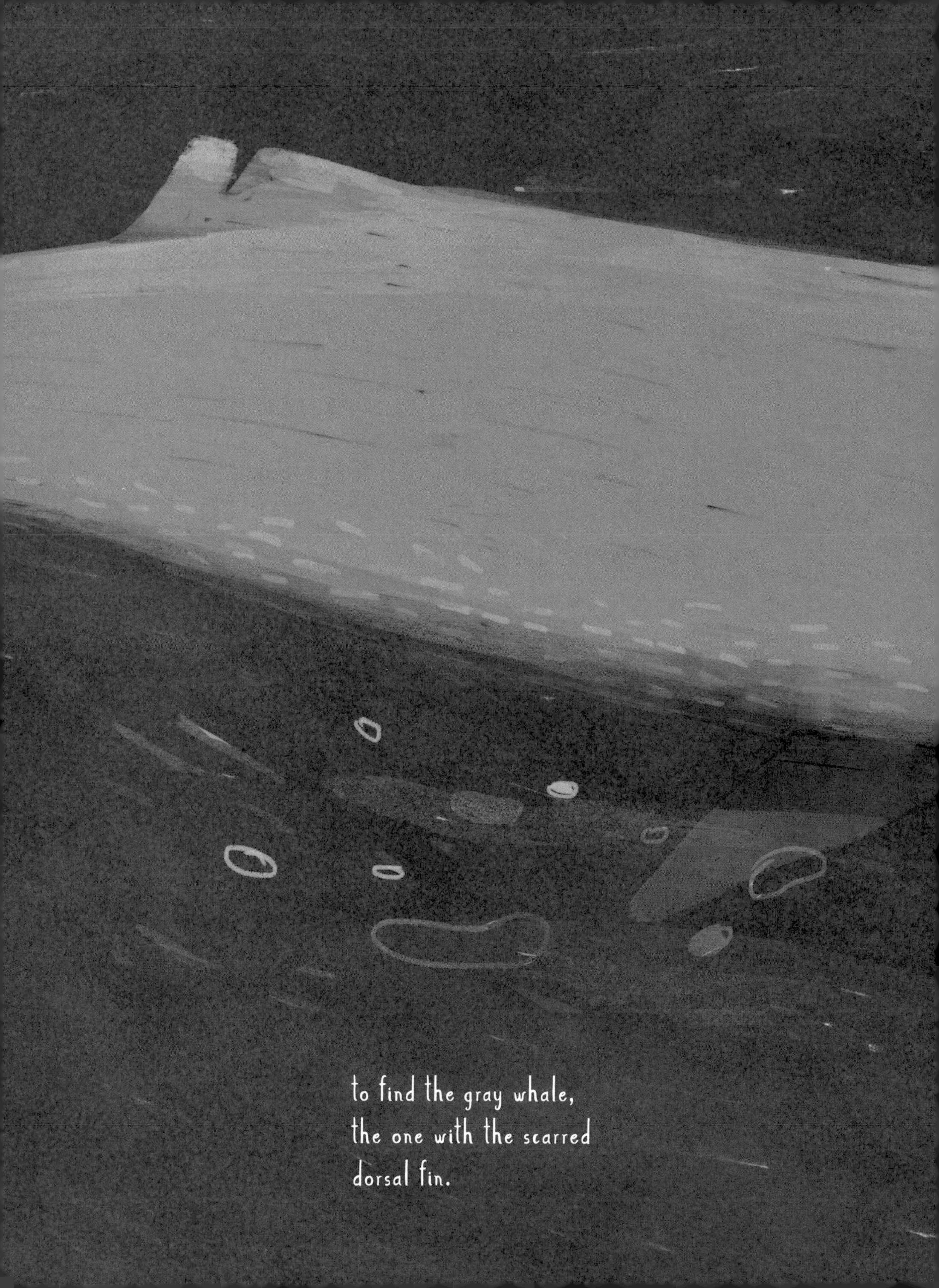

to find the gray whale,
the one with the scarred
dorsal fin.

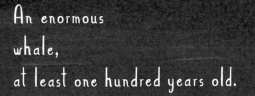

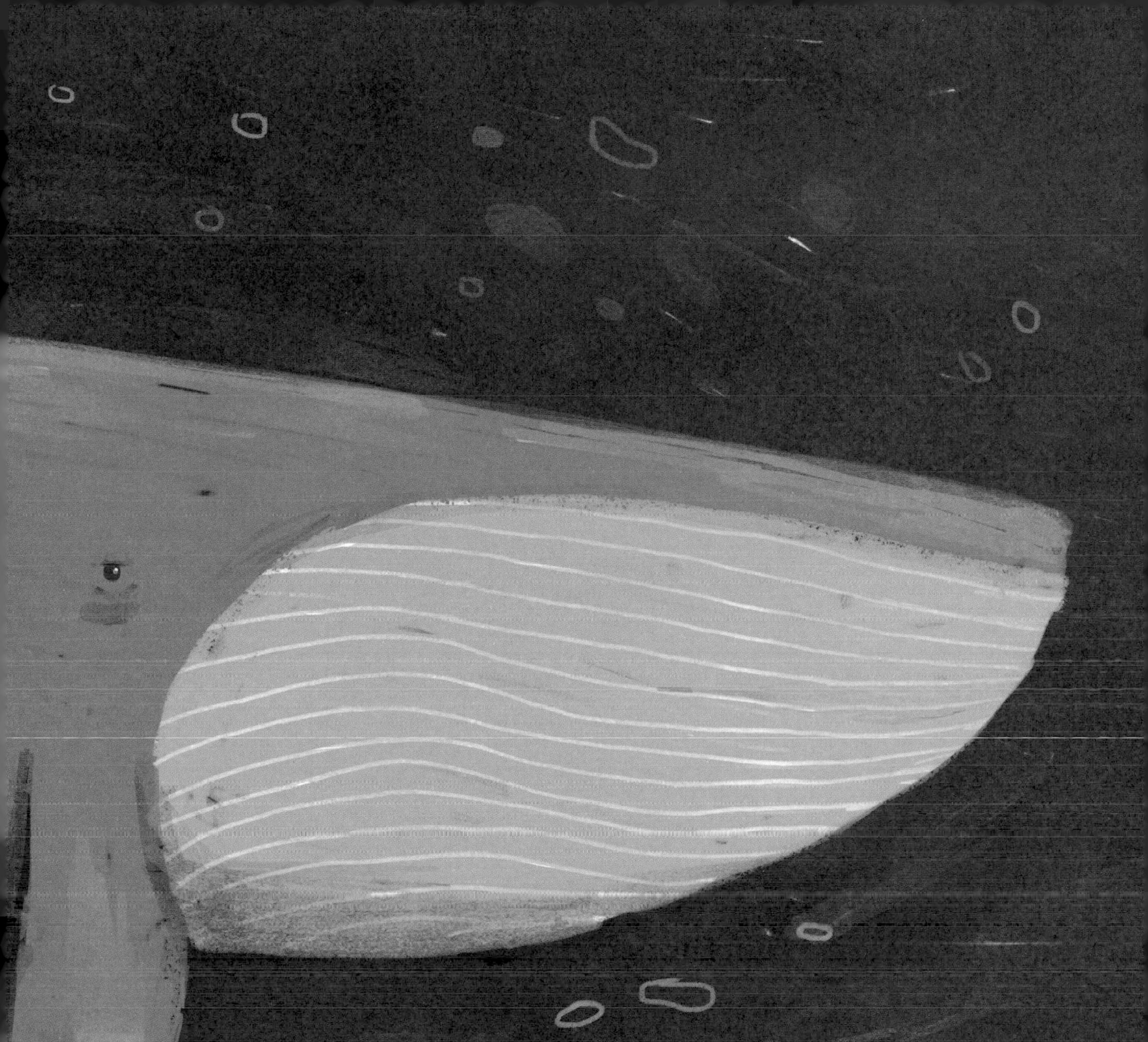

An enormous
whale,
at least one hundred years old.

For a long time,
the other fishermen would laugh.

They never missed a chance
to poke fun
at Jack.

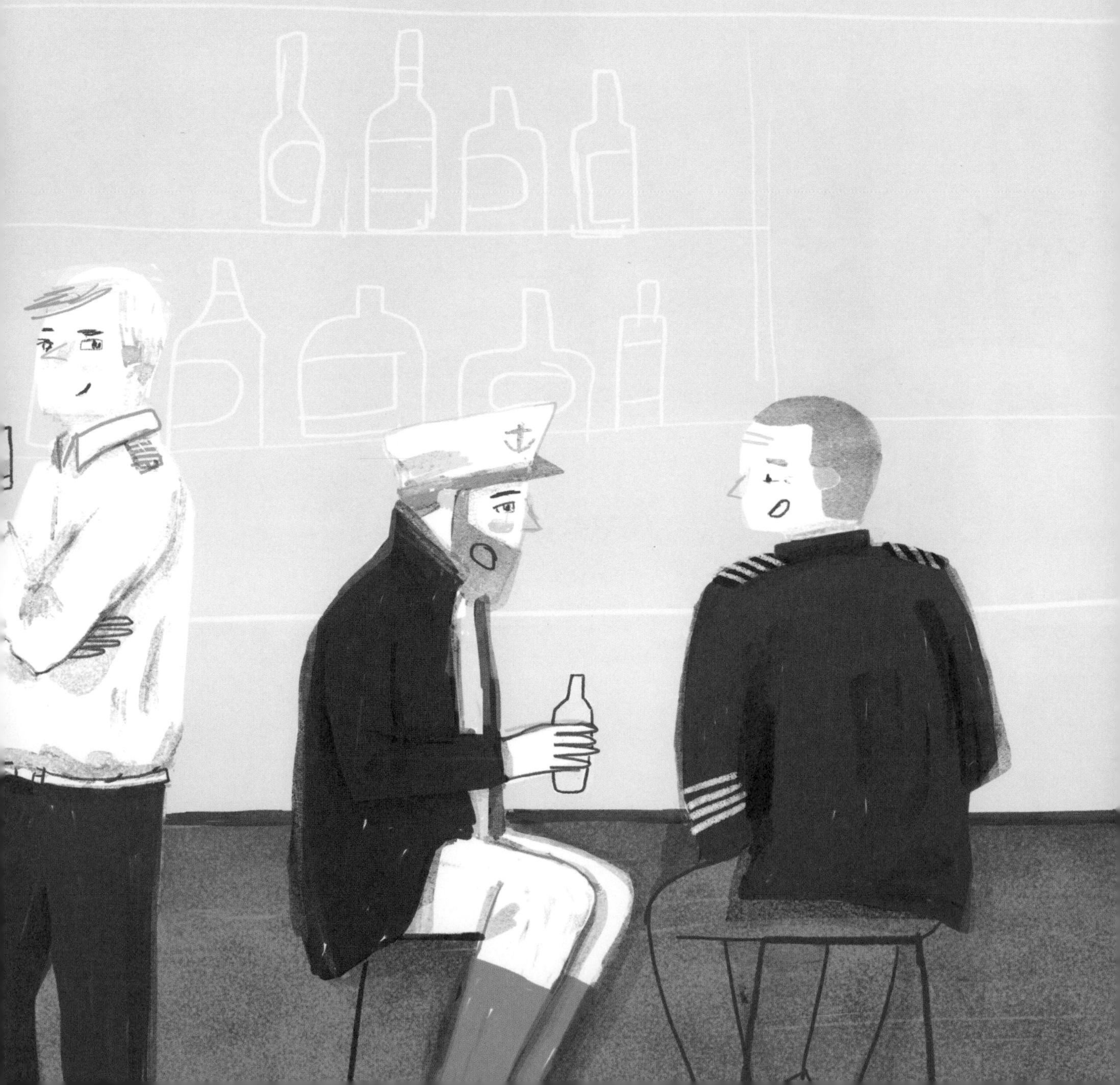

"There he is!"
"Attaboy, another big catch!"
"Hey, Jack! When will you catch that whale?"

Ho ho ho,
ha ha ha.

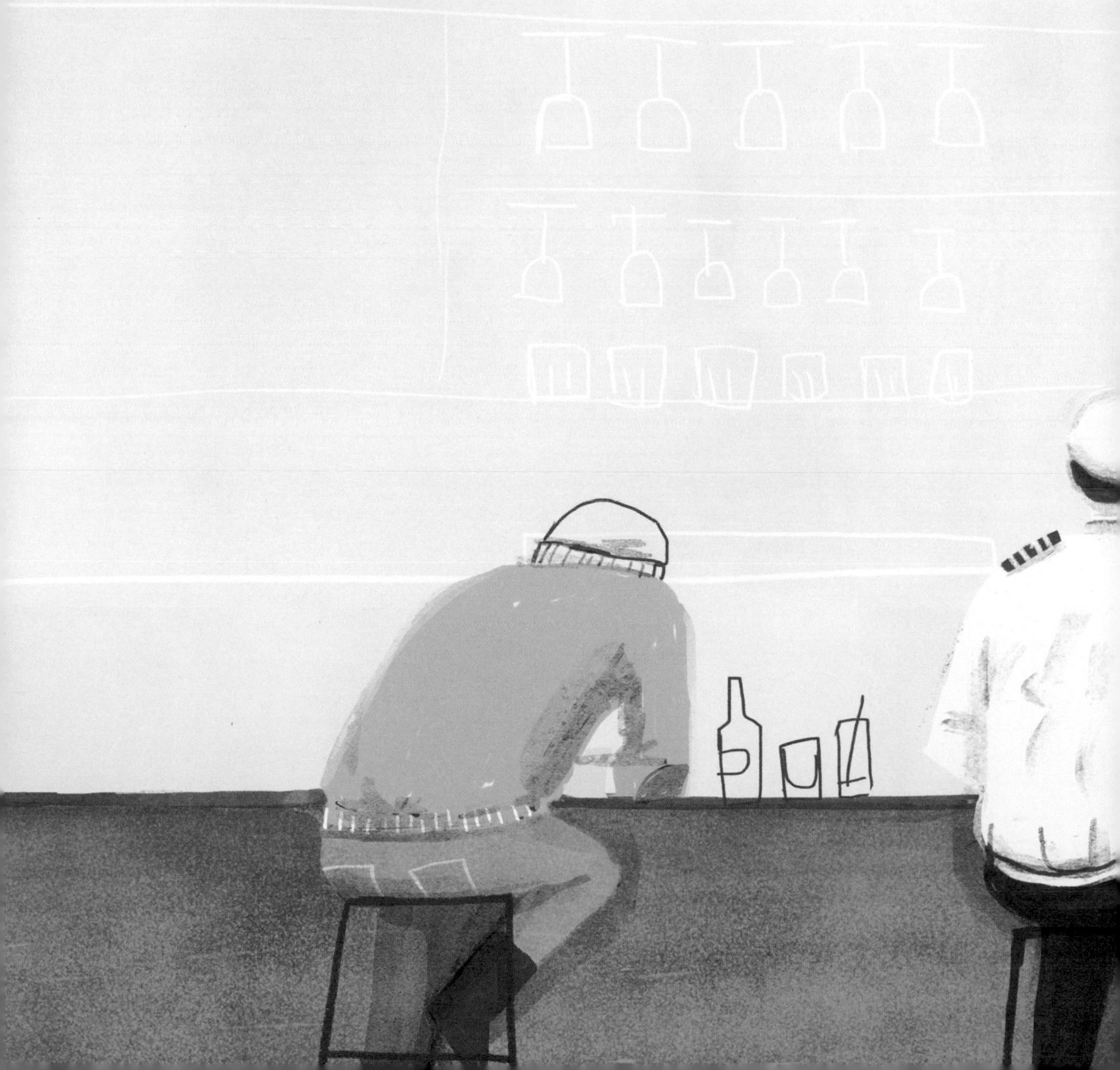

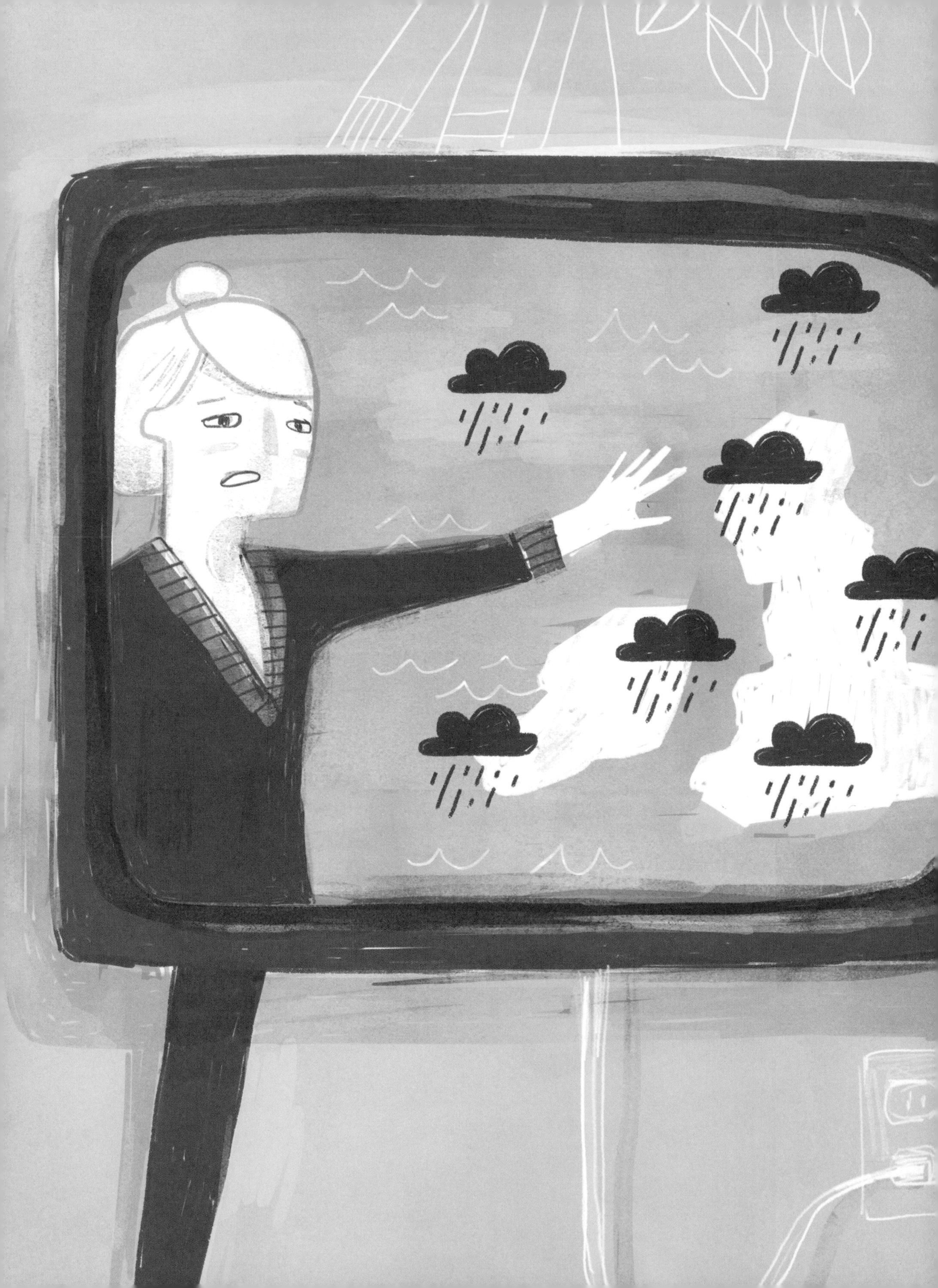

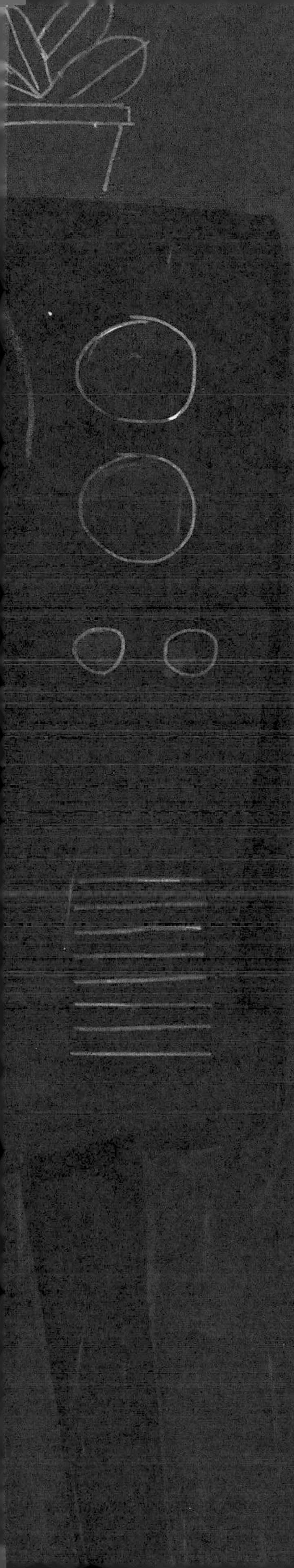

Until the day
it rained
buckets.

The rains ravaged
even the smallest bit of land

of each garden,
of each house,
of each village

for miles.

The fishermen and the other villagers,
who were very hungry,
asked Jack

(who had docked to see about
a damaged anchor)

to stop throwing back
the fish he caught

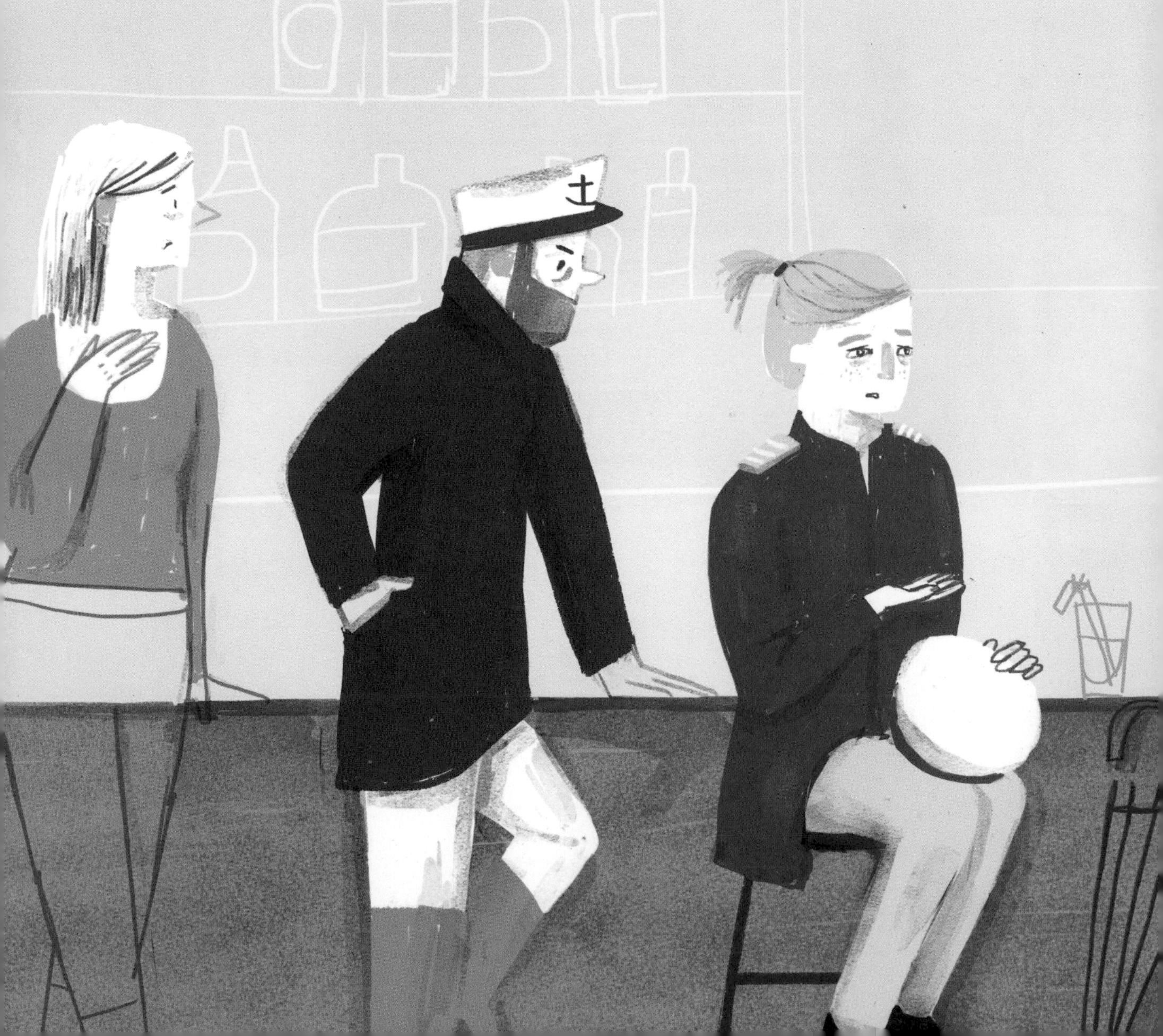

and to share
the vegetables and fruit that,
despite all the rain,
kept

growing
for some reason
on his boat
(where the sun beat down).

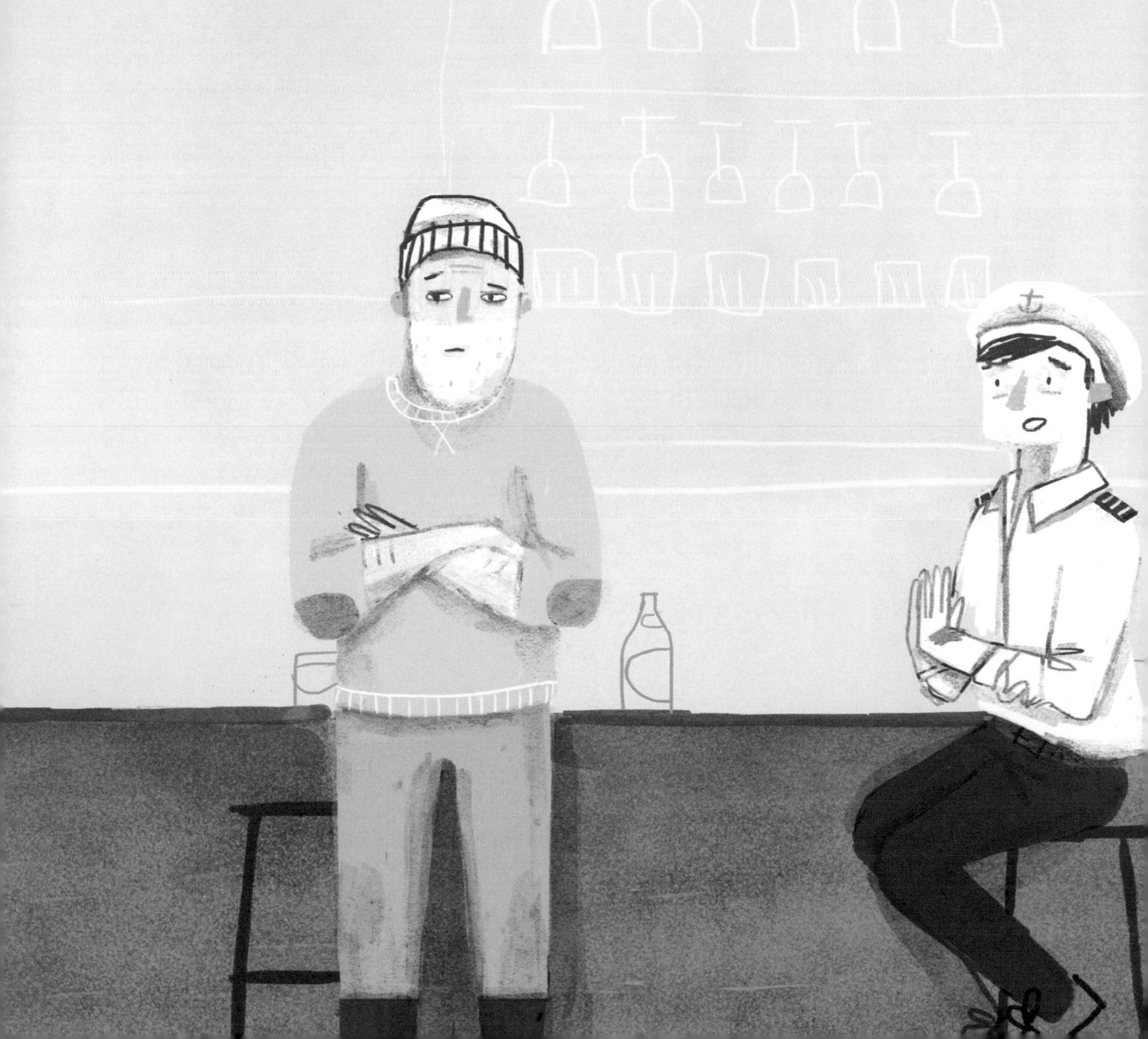

But Jack refused.
He knew that
without the fruit and vegetables
he would be forced
like them
to live

on land

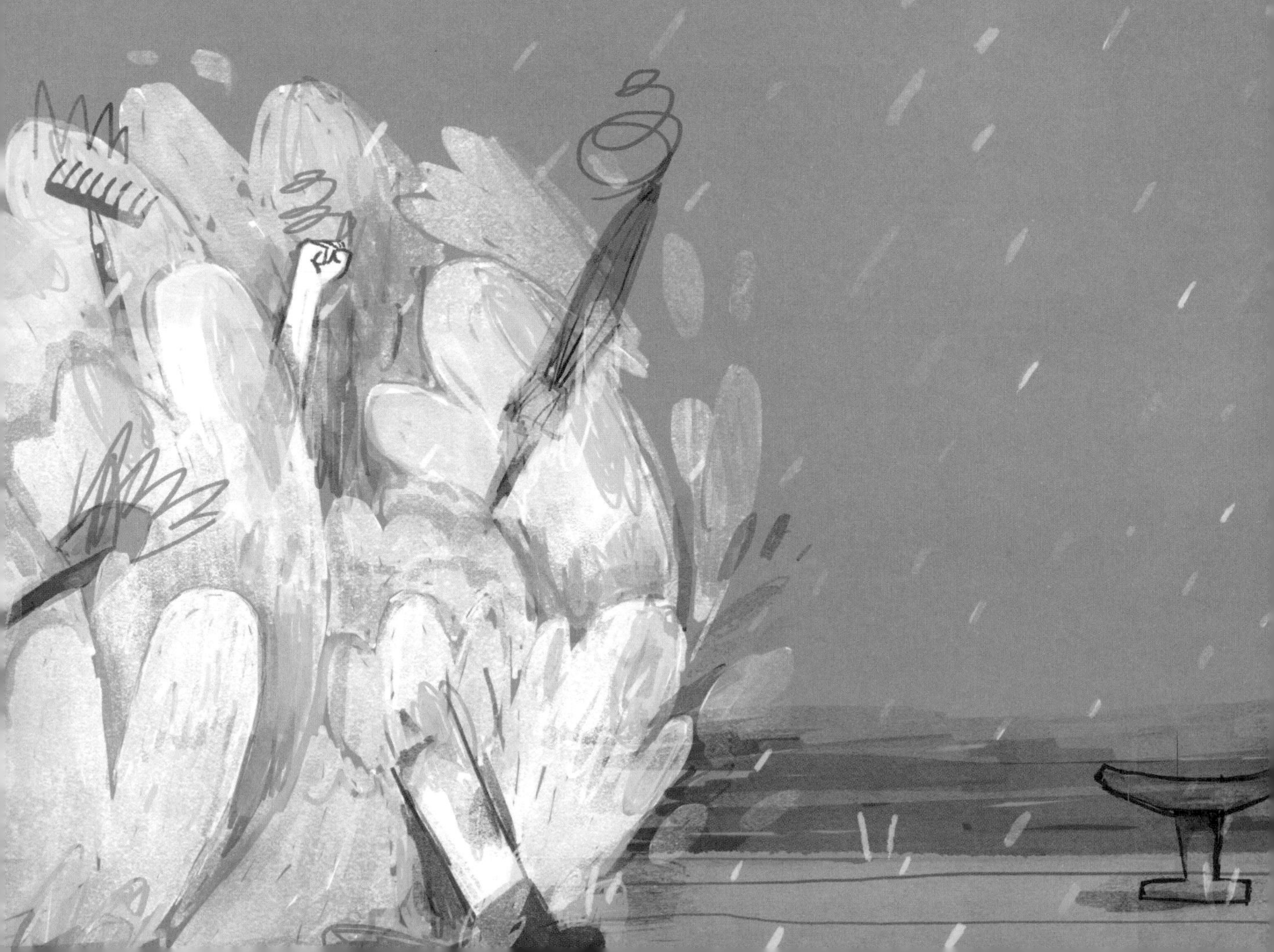

and would never find
the gray whale with the scarred
dorsal fin.

Ravenous,
the villagers
suddenly became angry with Jack,

who had to run
lickety-split
back to his boat and
avoid the beating.

Bats,
umbrellas,
and even broomsticks.

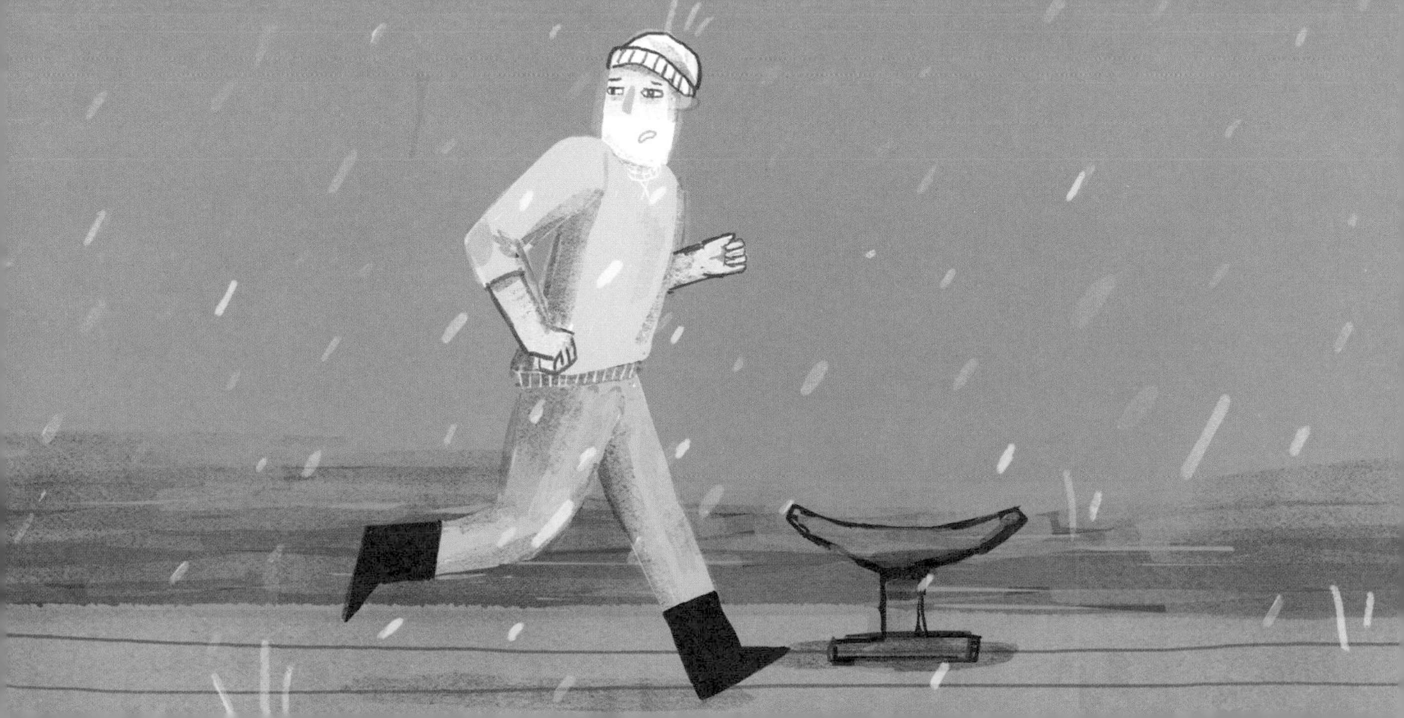

After weighing anchor,
Jack knew that he would
never set foot on land

and that from now on
the sea would be
his only

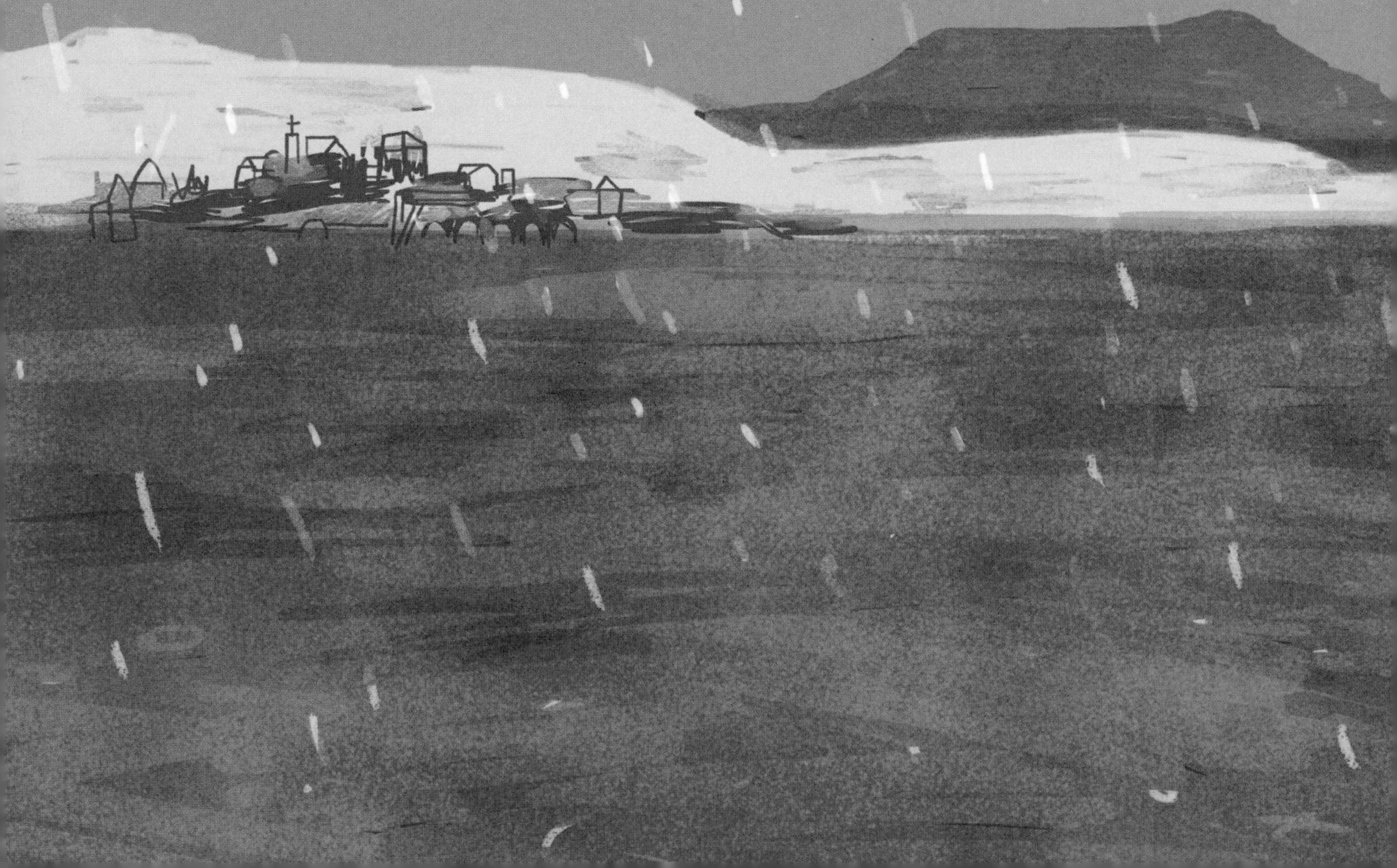

home.

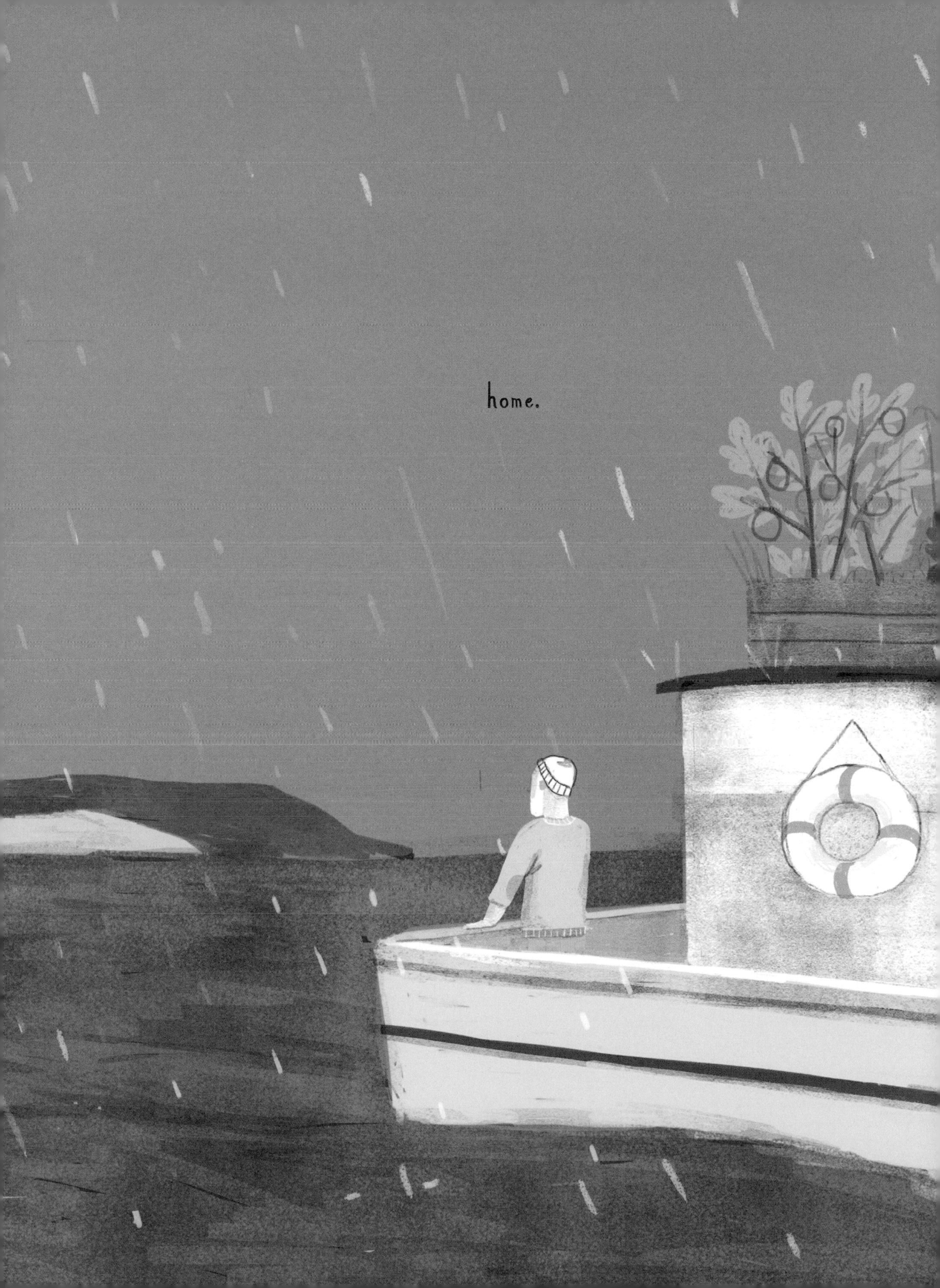

It is possible to get lost on water,
on land,
or in the air.

It is possible to get lost
in too much noise

or
not enough.

It is possible to get lost
pretty much anywhere,
actually.

And one thing is certain:
it was on his boat
that Jack lost himself.

Or at least,
forgot himself.

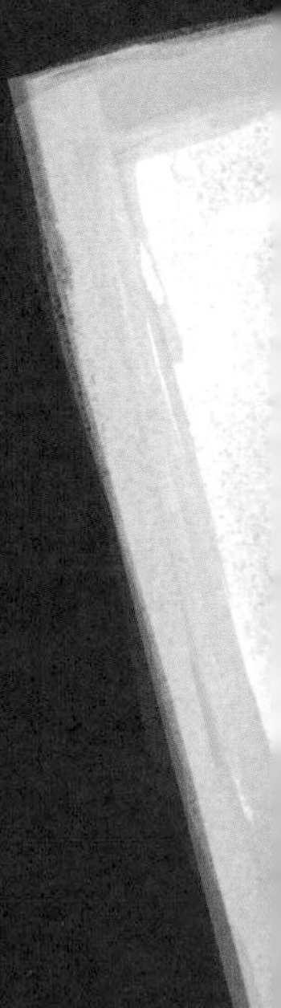

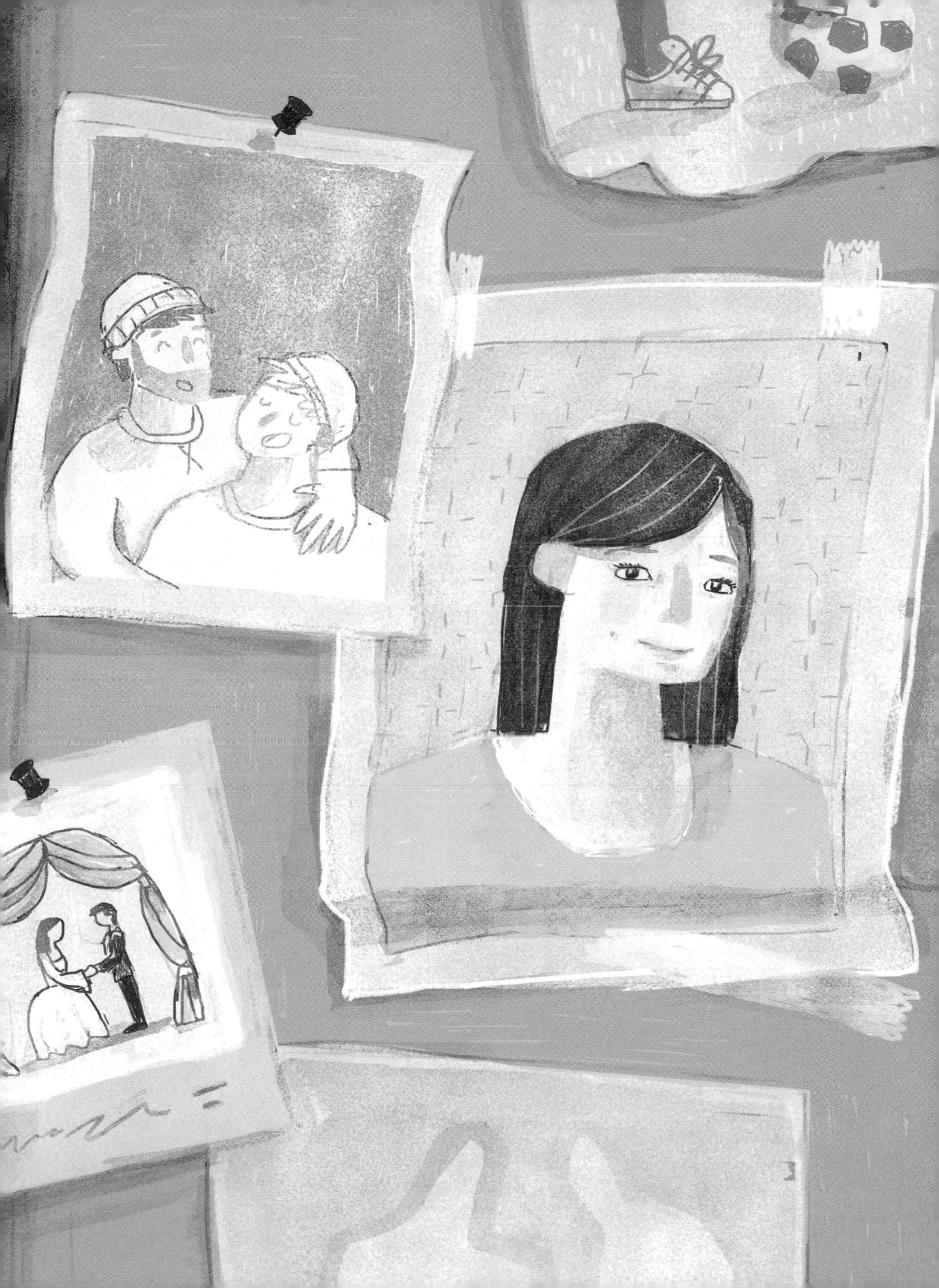

Before becoming
a lonely,
grouchy sailor

everyone had come to dislike,

Jack had been a good man,
the kind of man it's hard to find
nowadays.

Back then,
Jack had
everything he needed

to be happy.

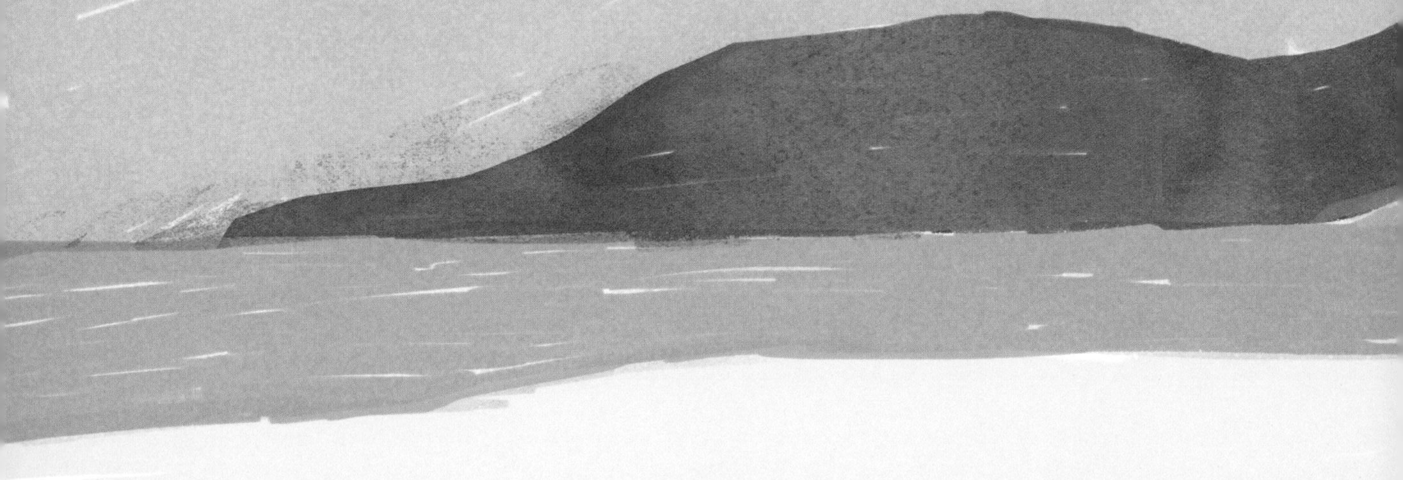

A wife who was
just sweet enough

and a son
who was his carbon copy (minus the beard)
and who was dearer to him

than his own life.

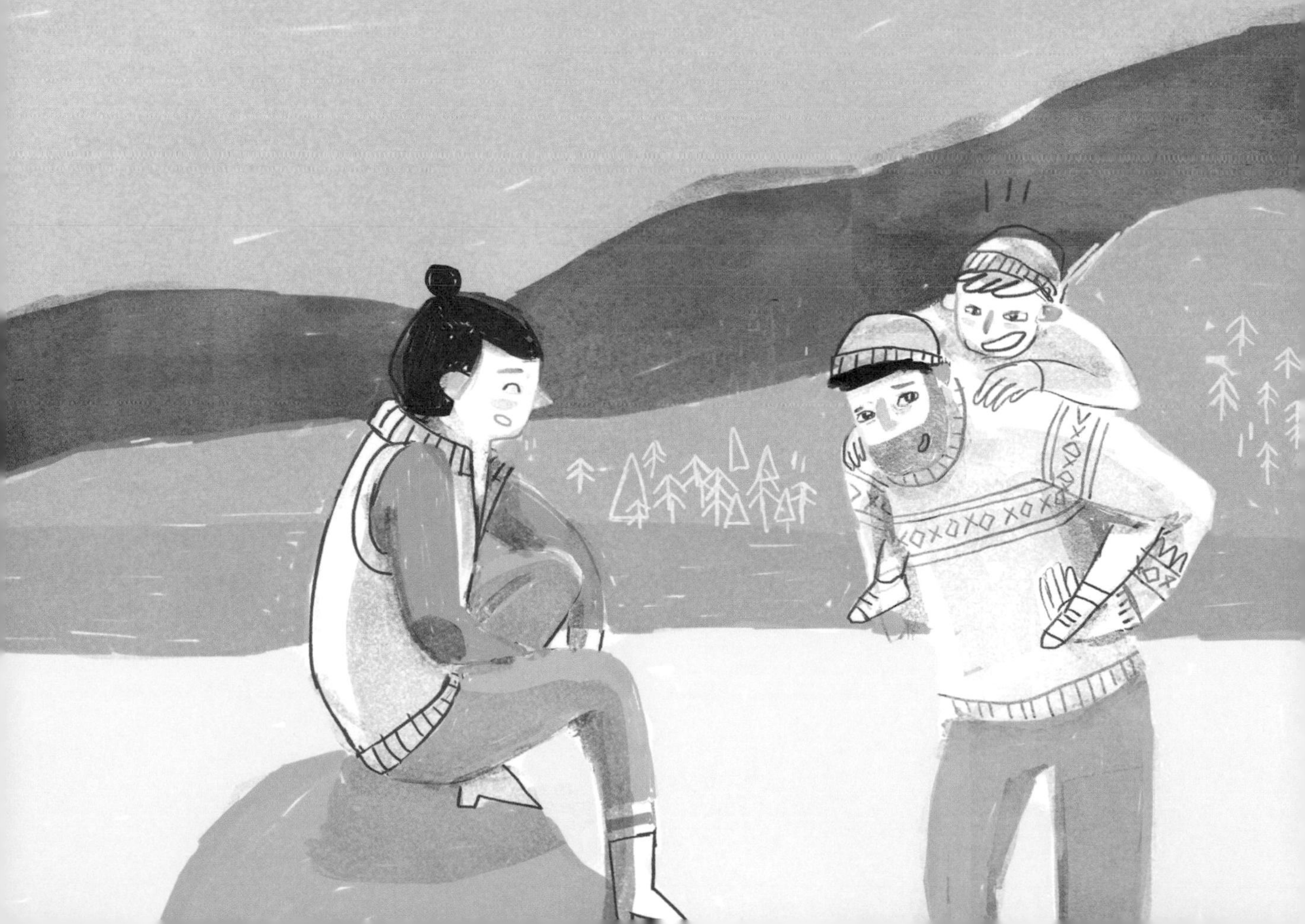

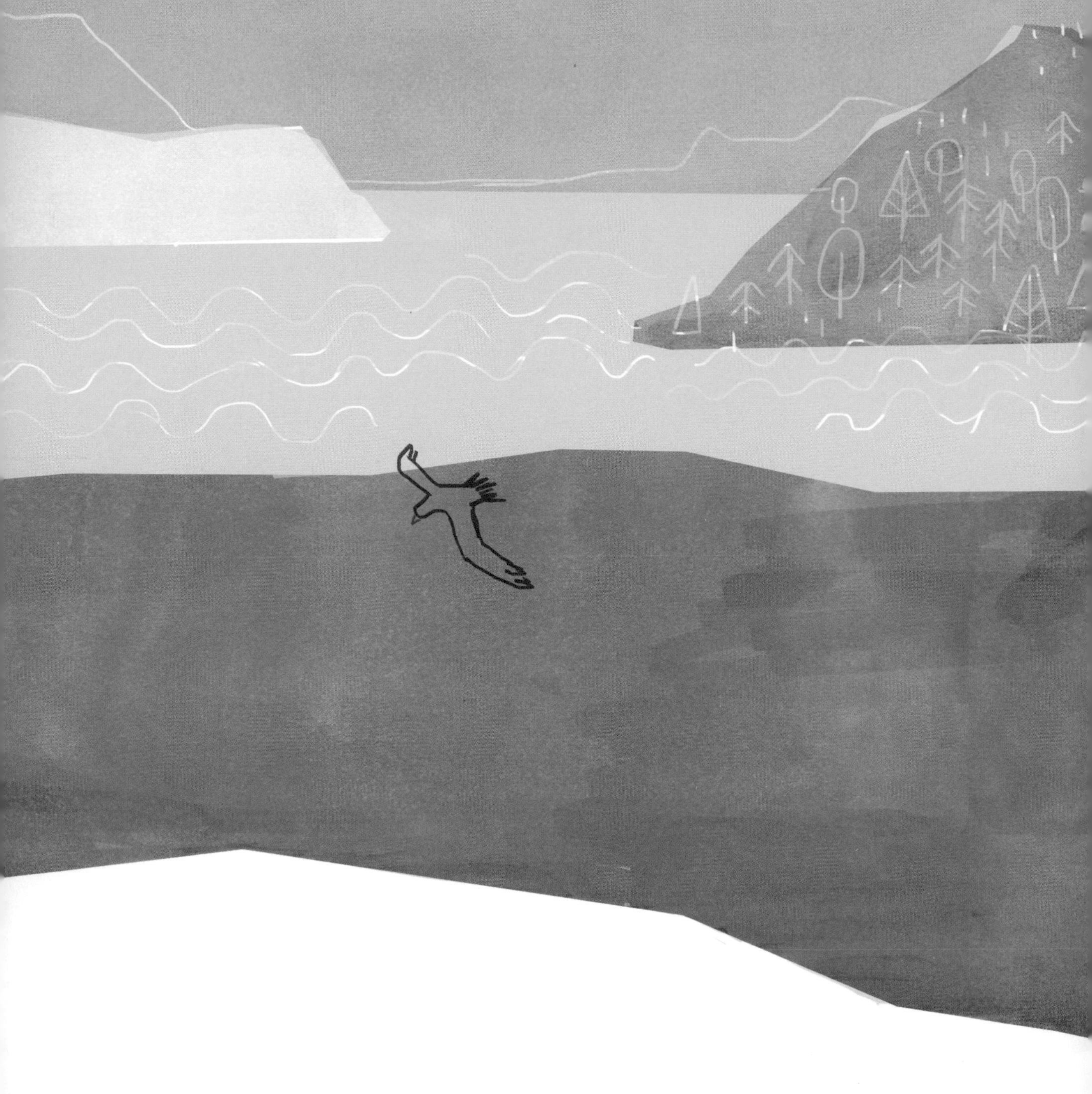

Jack brought Julos
everywhere
he went.

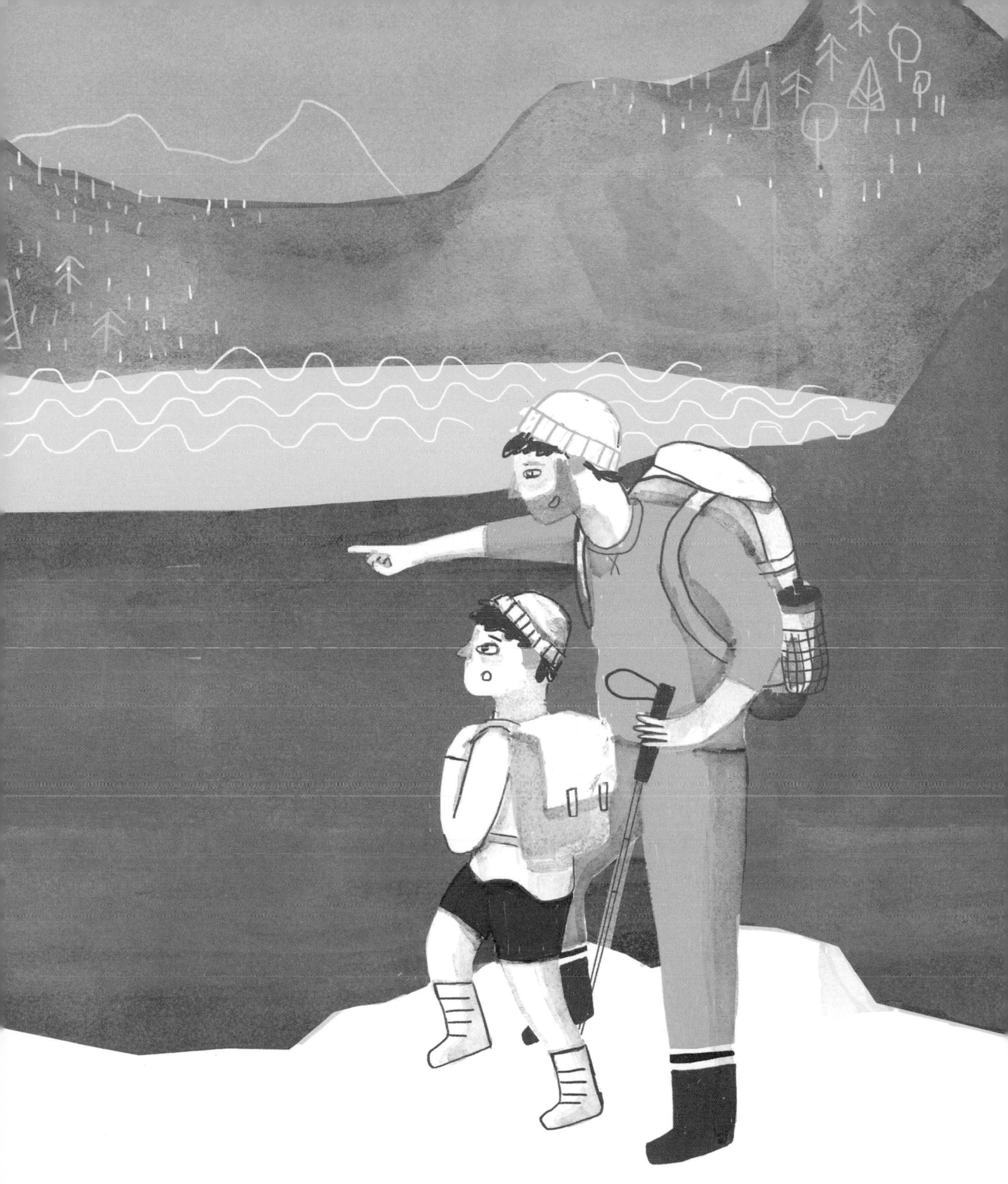

Everywhere.

Until the day
his life
was upended.

It happened at dawn.

Jack's boat
was still shrouded
in mist

when he opened his eyes
and saw
that Julos had

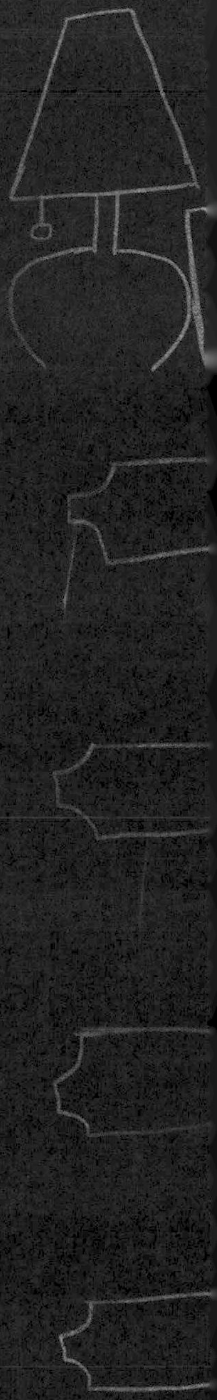

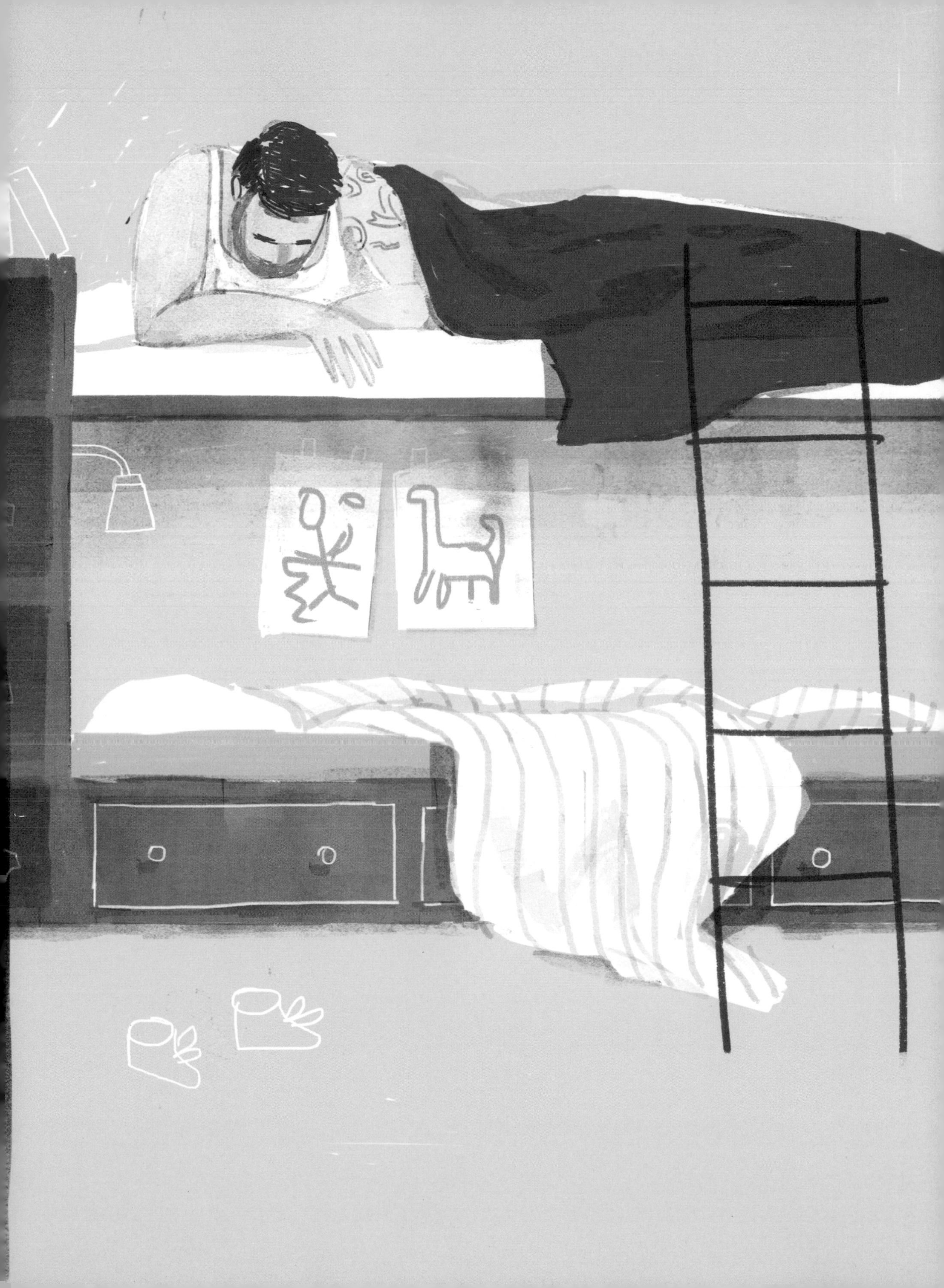

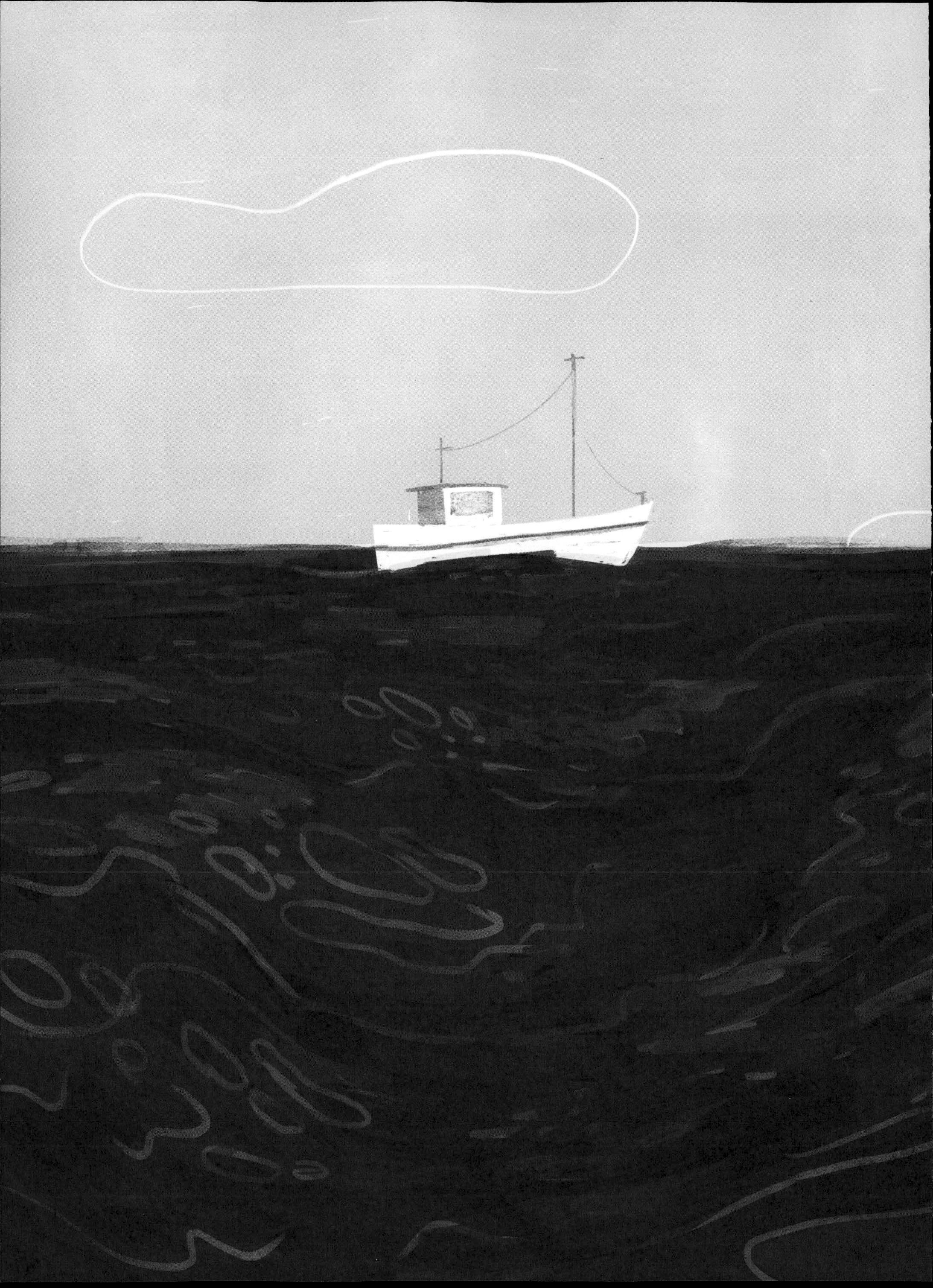

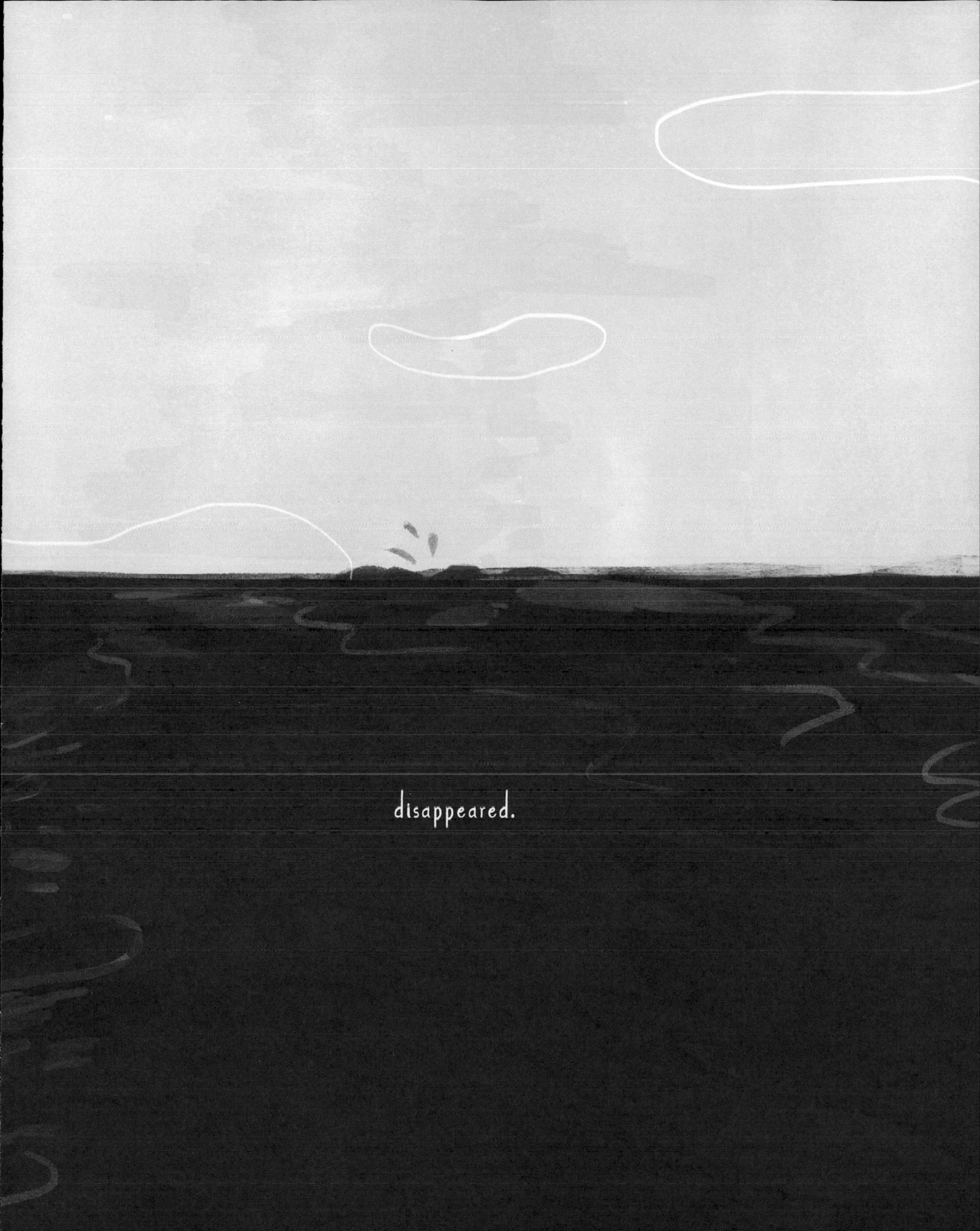
disappeared.

Impossible, Jack thought.
People do not disappear like that—
poof—
and certainly not

on a boat.

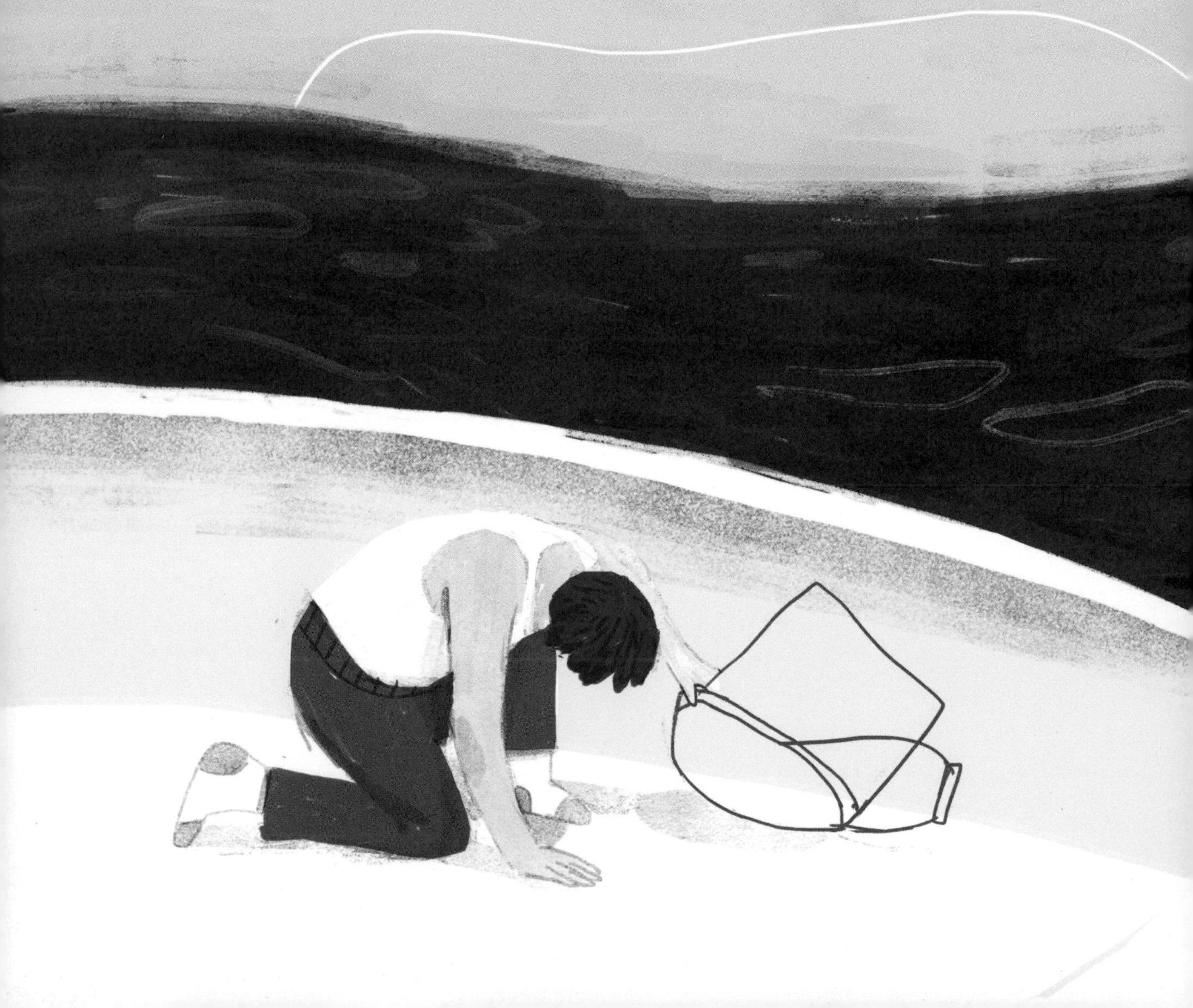

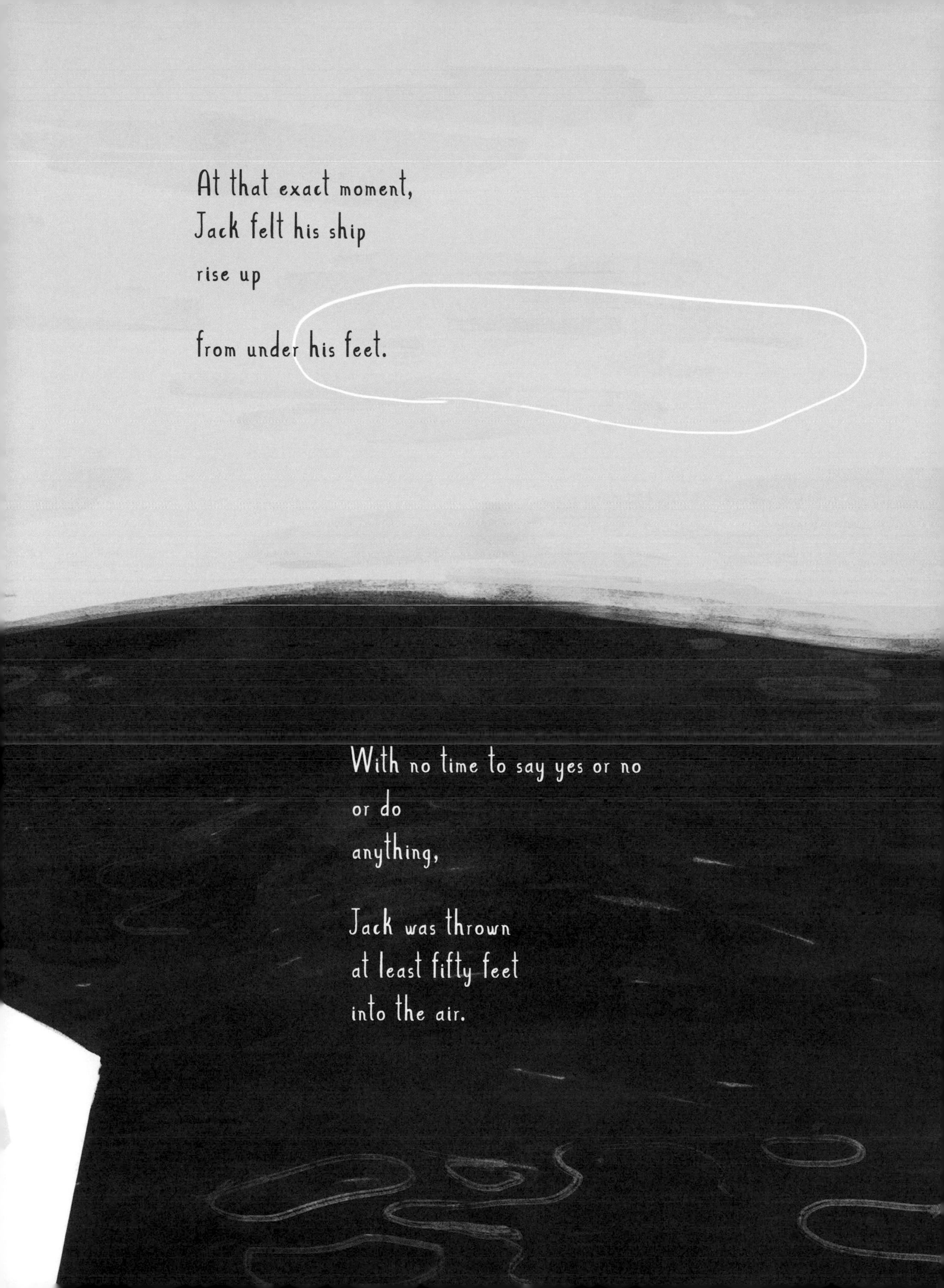

At that exact moment,
Jack felt his ship
rise up

from under his feet.

With no time to say yes or no
or do
anything,

Jack was thrown
at least fifty feet
into the air.

That's when,
as he flew for the first
and last time in his life,

without knowing where and when he would land,

Jack saw
for the first and (possibly)
last time in his life

the gray whale with the scarred
dorsal fin.

Through a tangle of
fear,
dizziness,
and terror,

Jack glimpsed
his son

in the beast's mouth.

His
Julos
swallowed up by a whale.

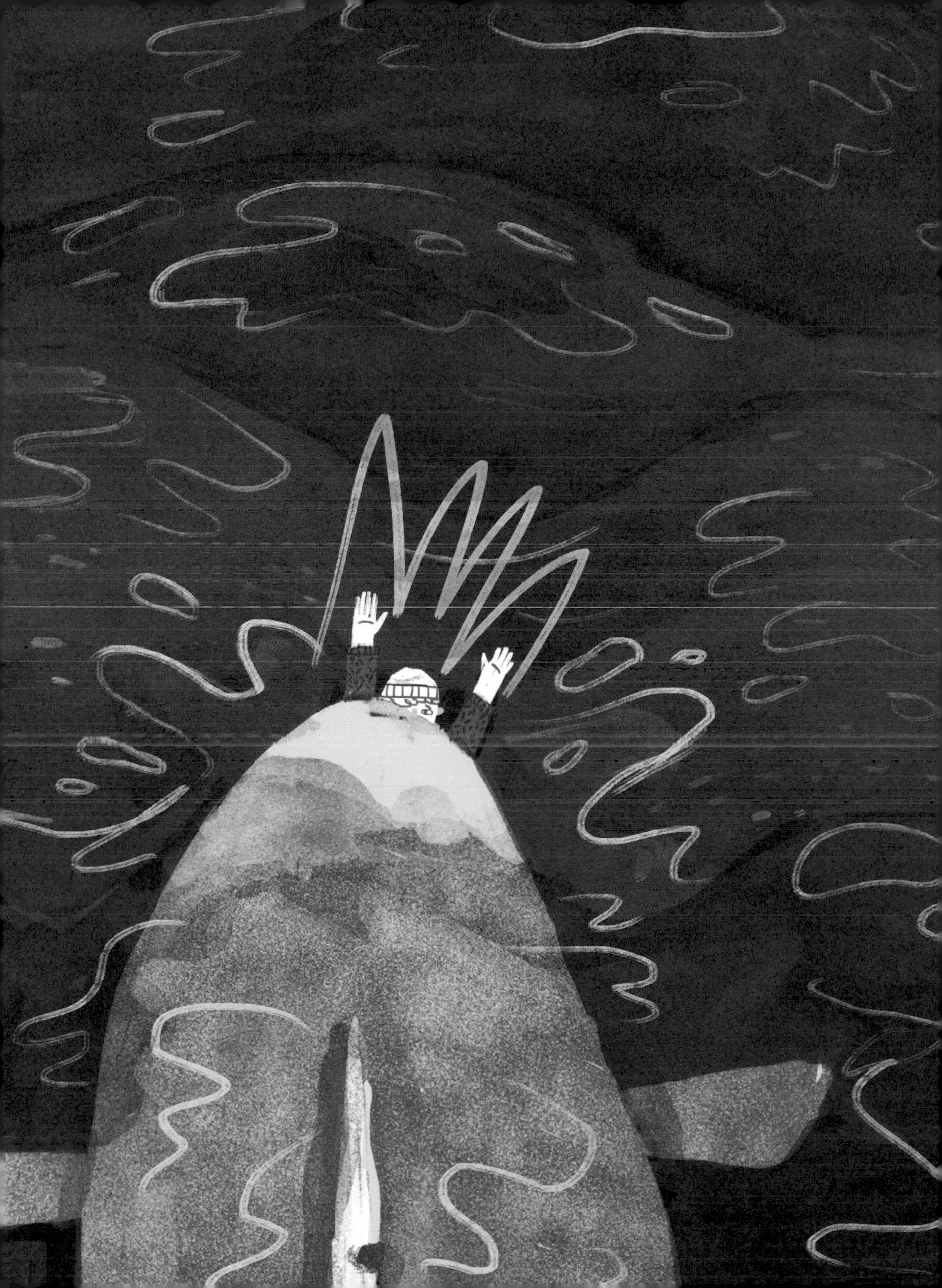

Jack did not feel cold
or pain
as his body hit
the water,
still choppy in the beast's wake.

And as it swam away
he began to splash around
and

shout.

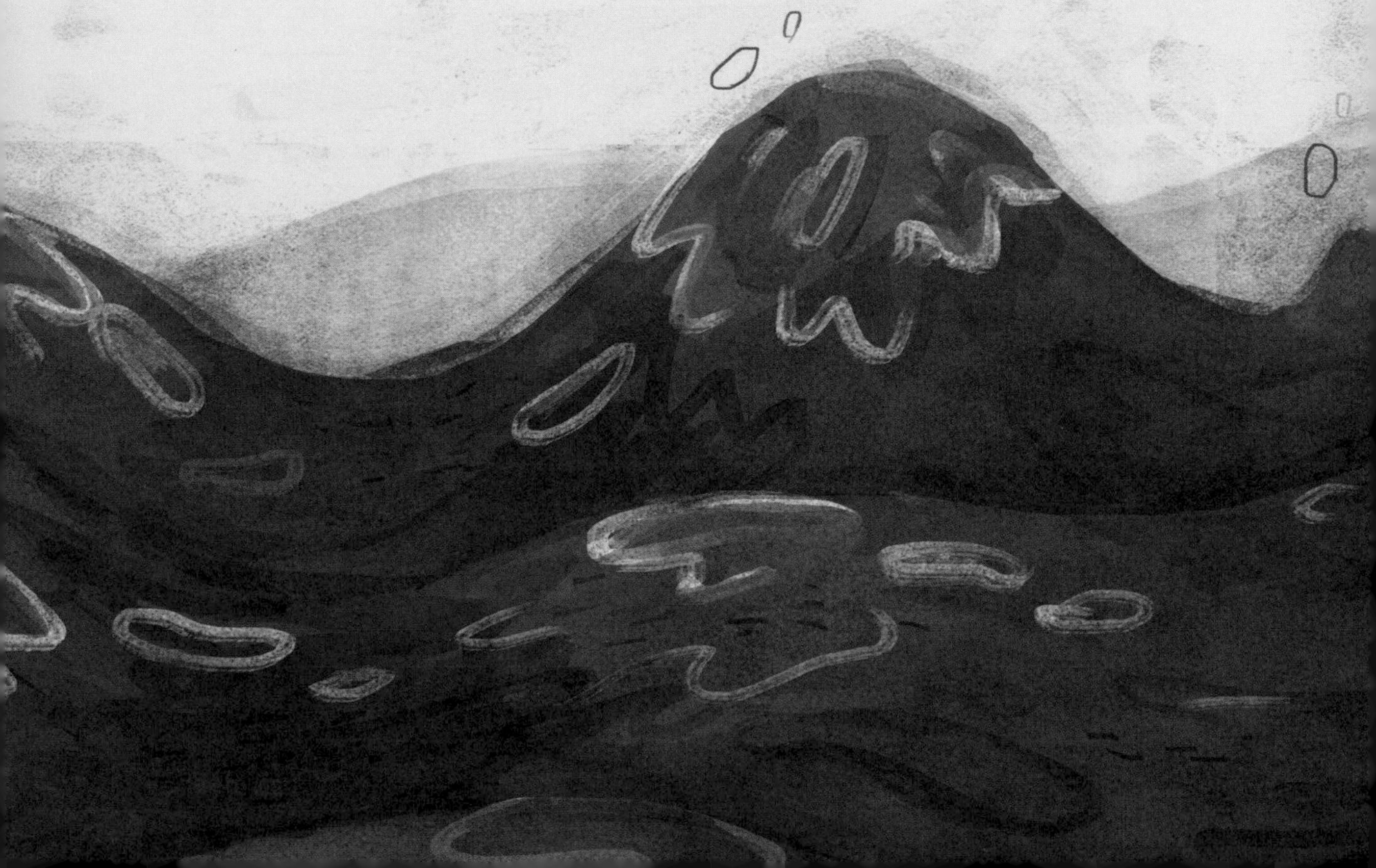

"BRING BACK MY SON! YOU CAN'T DO THIS! I'LL FIND YOU!"

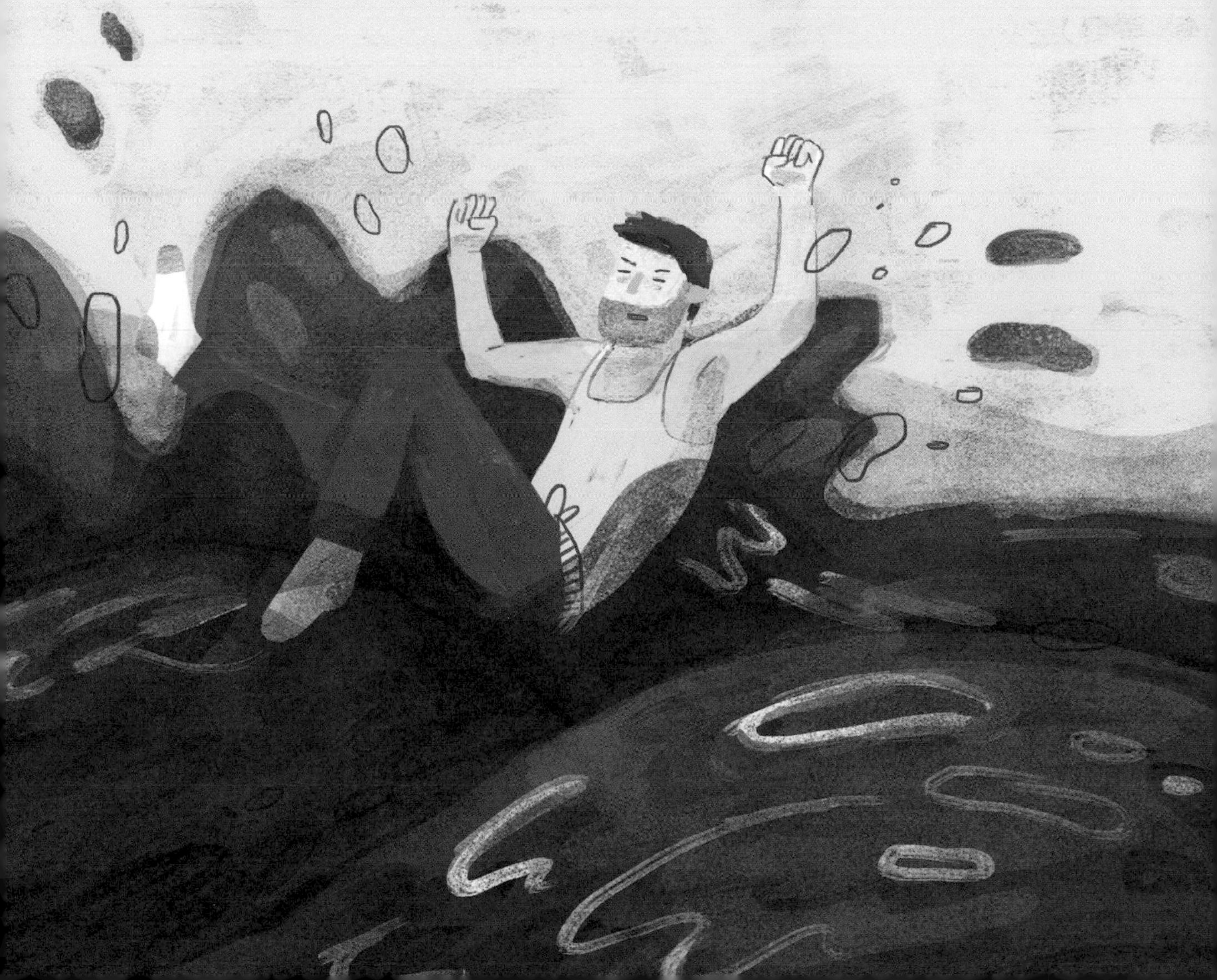

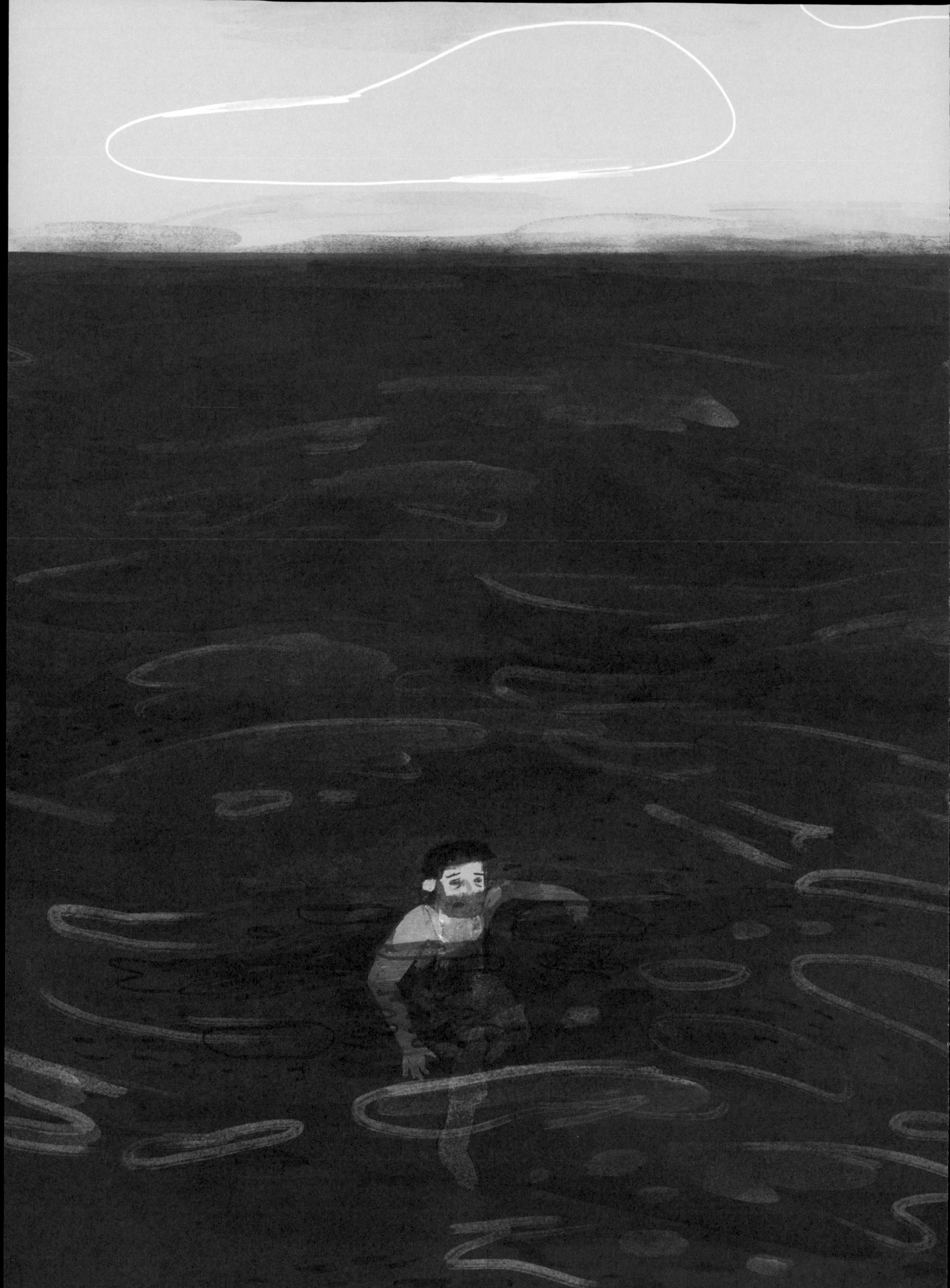

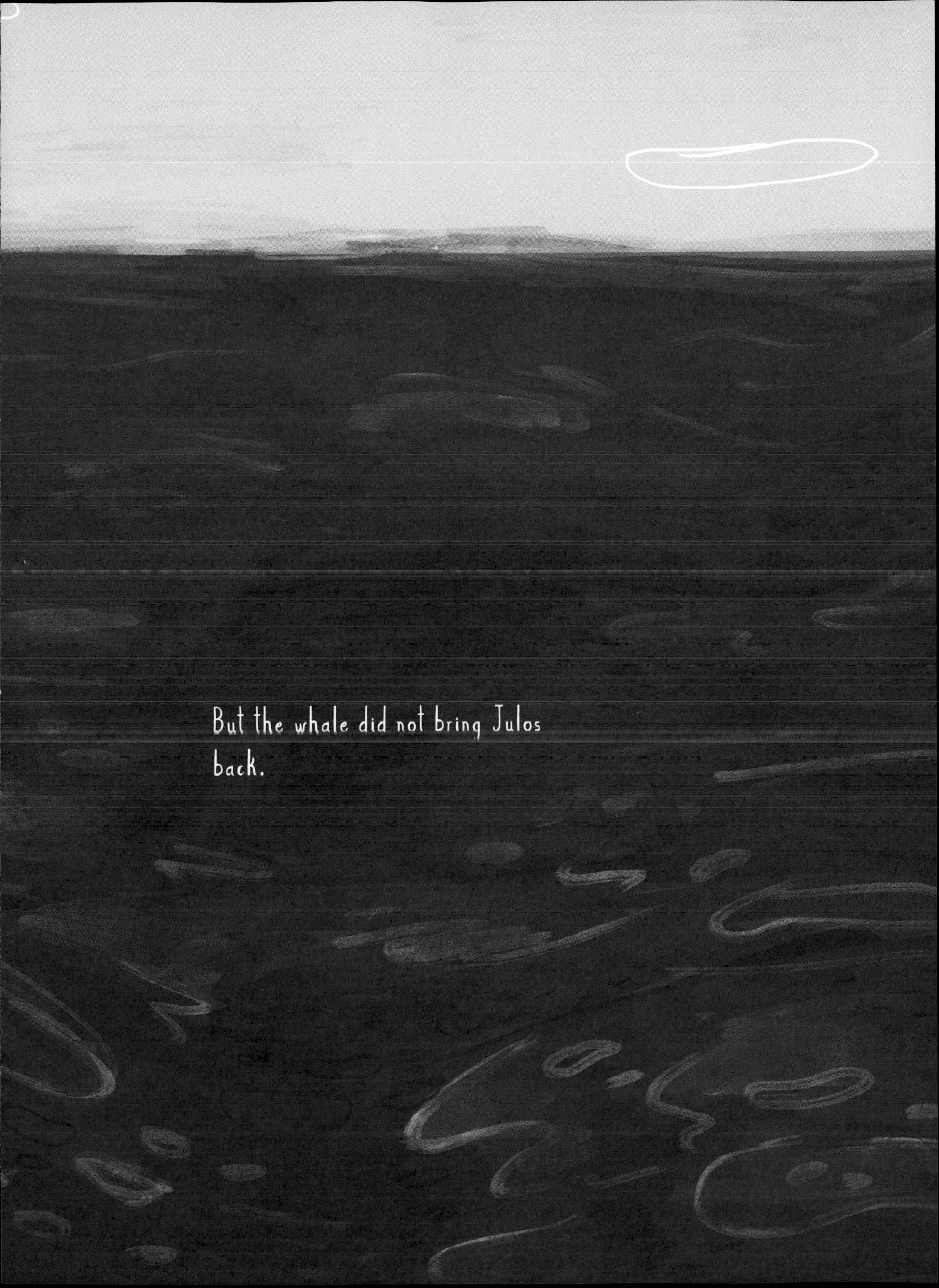

But the whale did not bring Julos
back.

So
Jack spent sixteen days and sixteen nights
there
on his boat

searching
in vain
and thinking of

his wife,

wondering if he should
return
and tell her everything
or remain at sea
and say nothing.

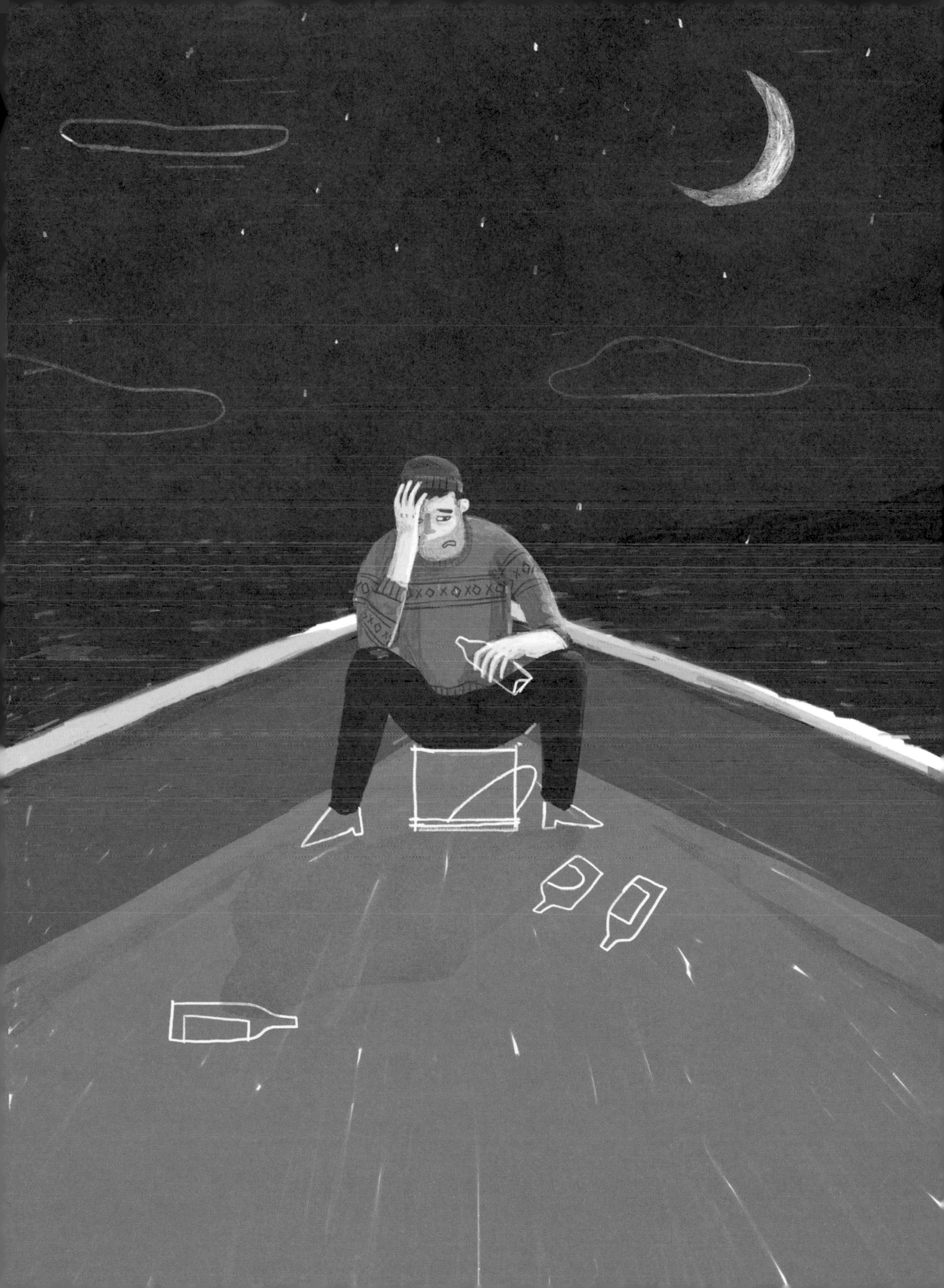

On the sixteenth night
Jack decided
that he would not

return.

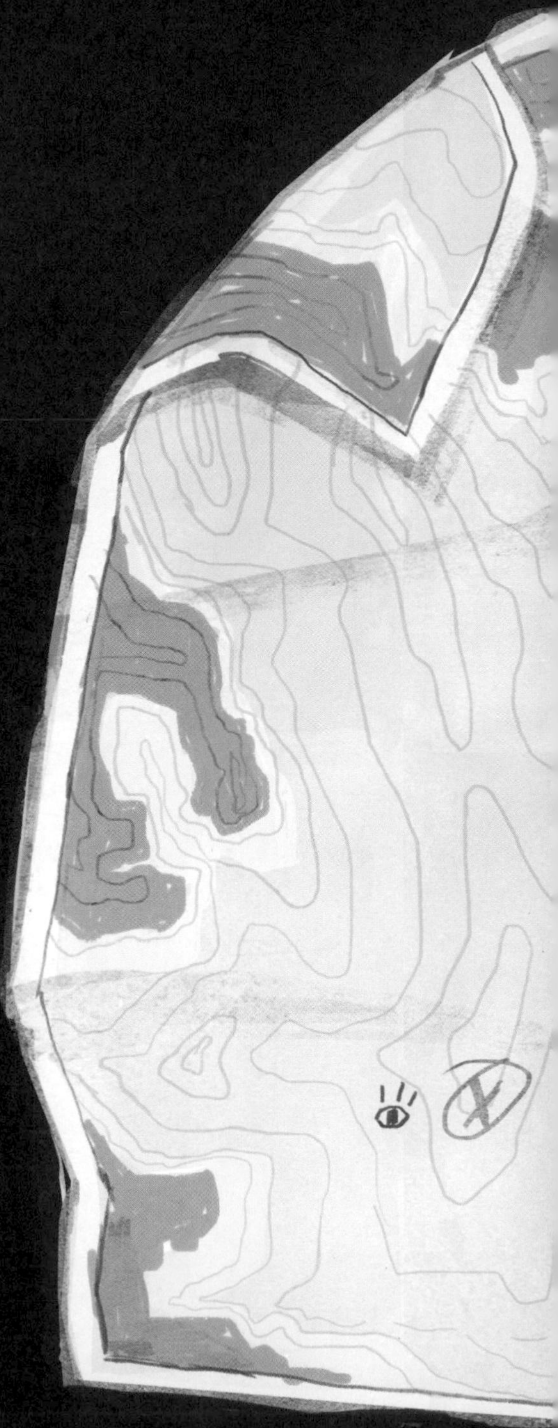

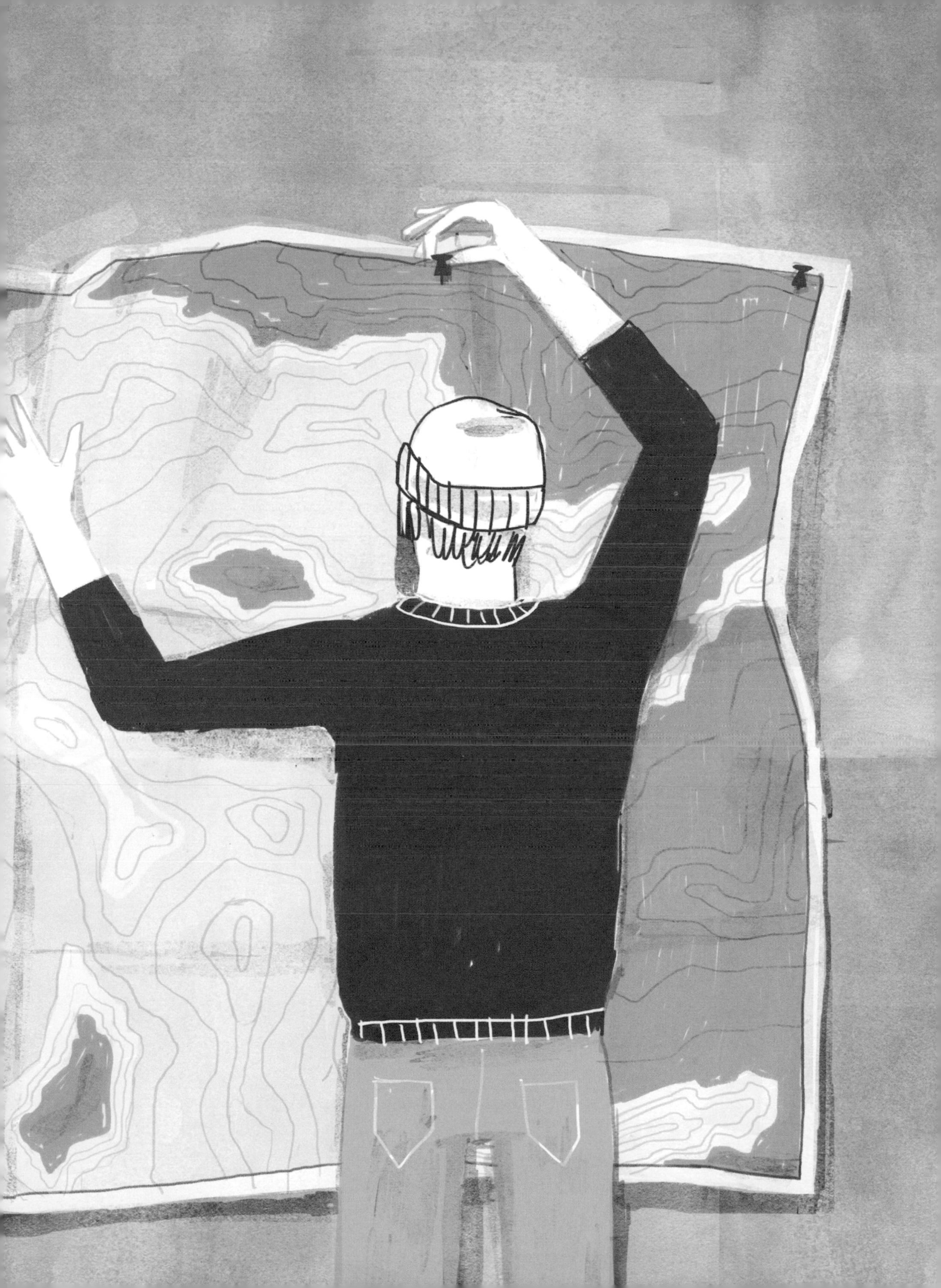

Not without
Julos.

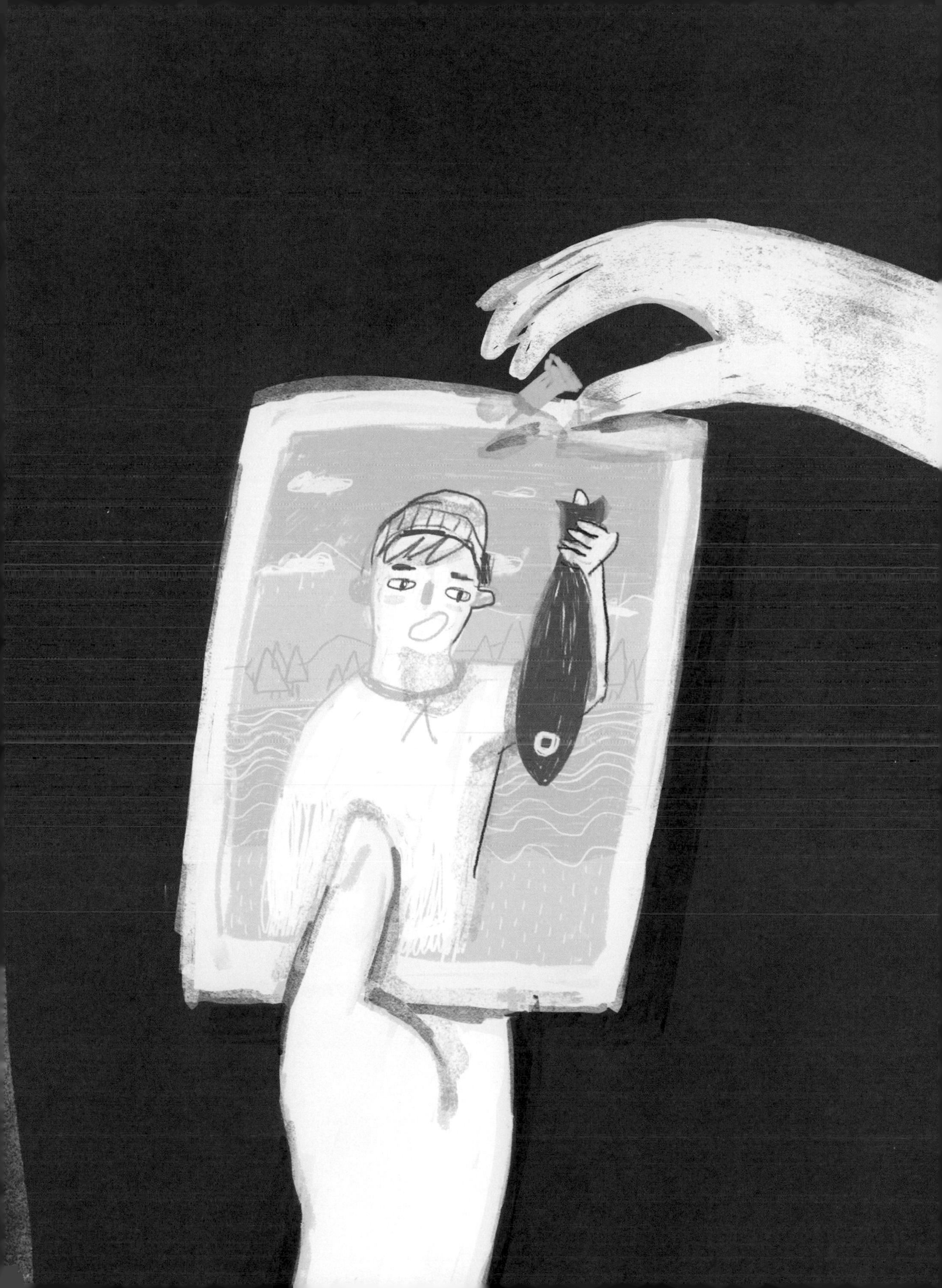

And that is how
in the most deafening silence,
the heart of the woman he loved

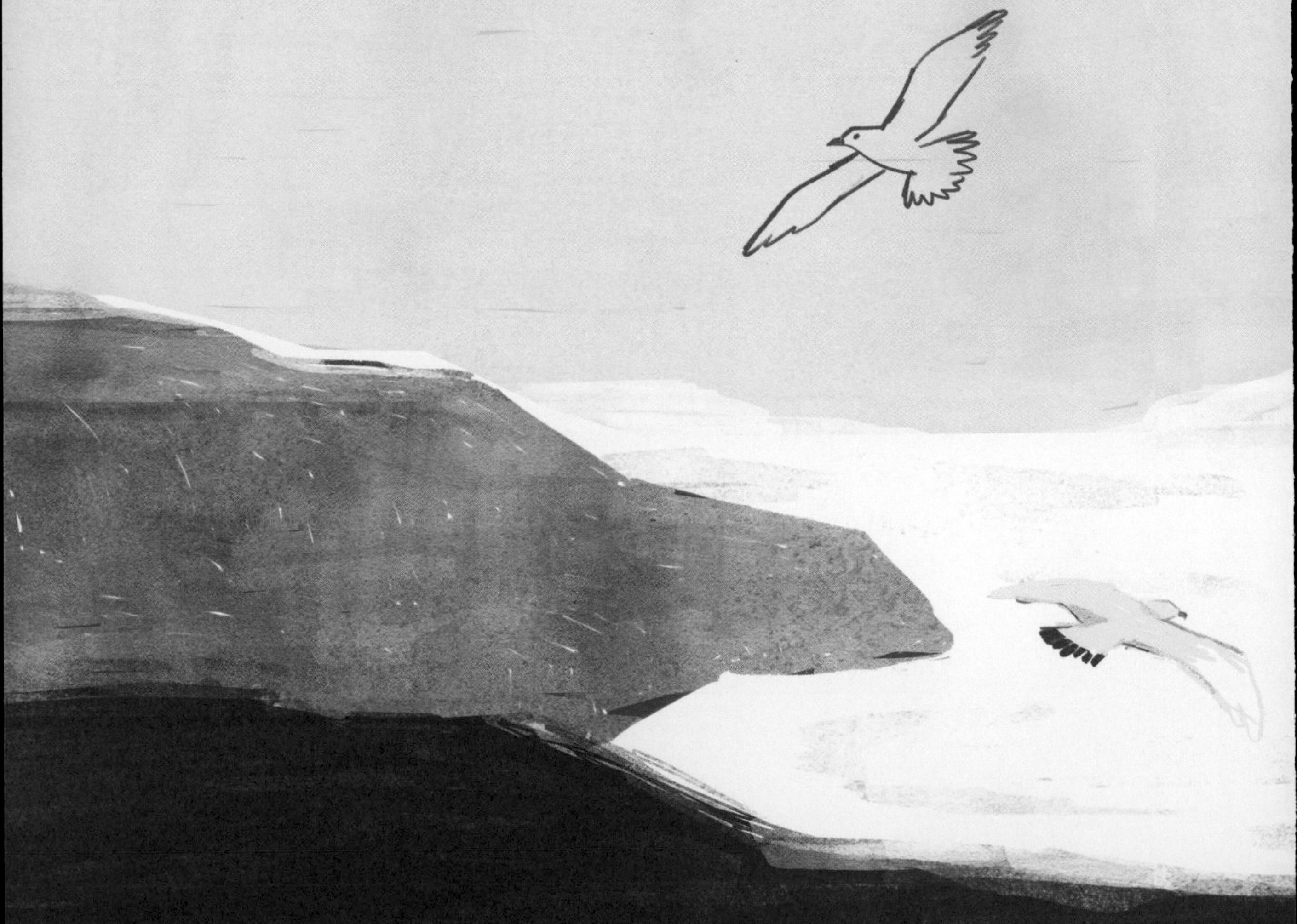

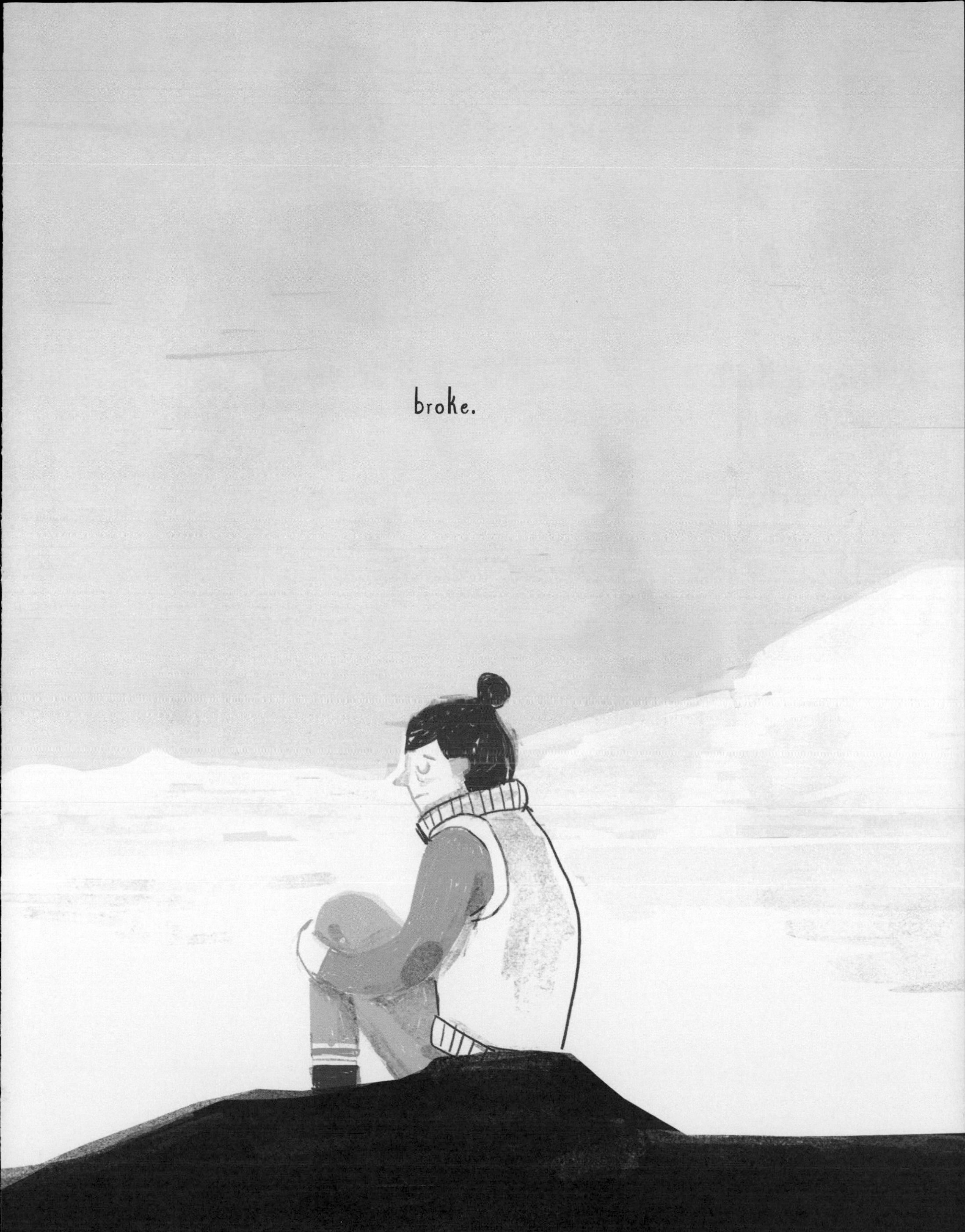
broke.

Many summers,
springs,
falls,
and of course winters
passed

before Jack
saw
the gray whale with the scarred
dorsal fin.

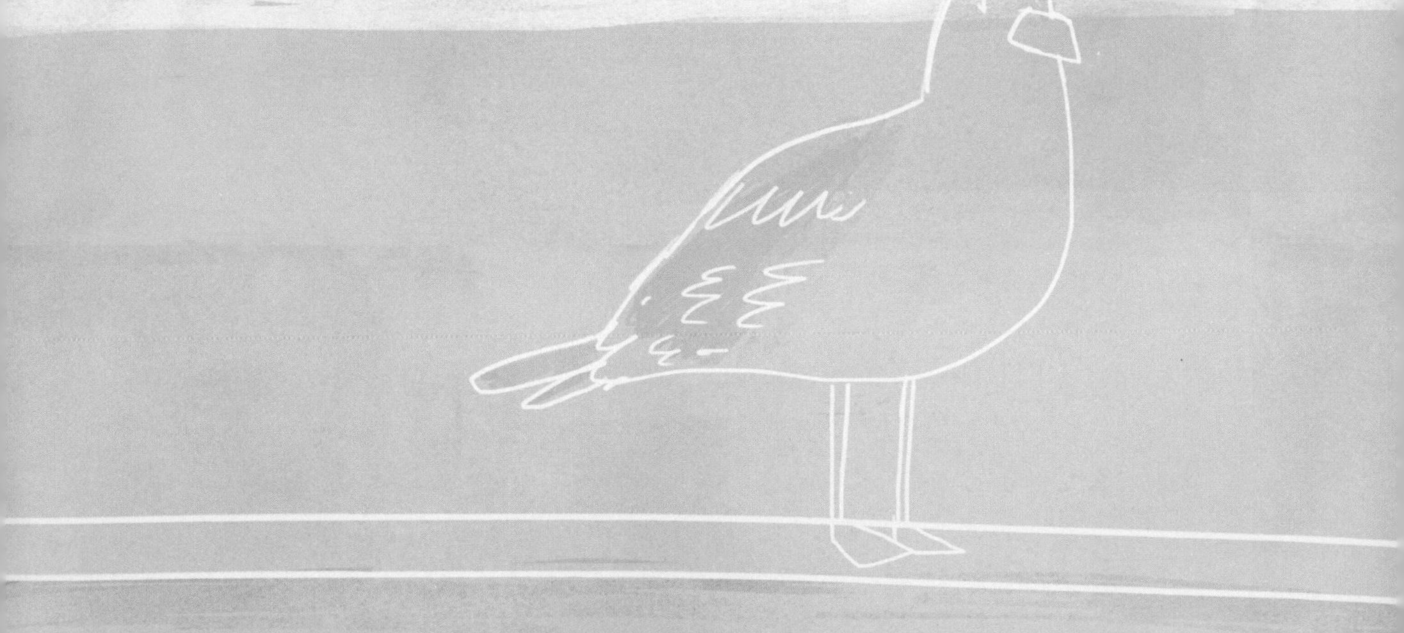

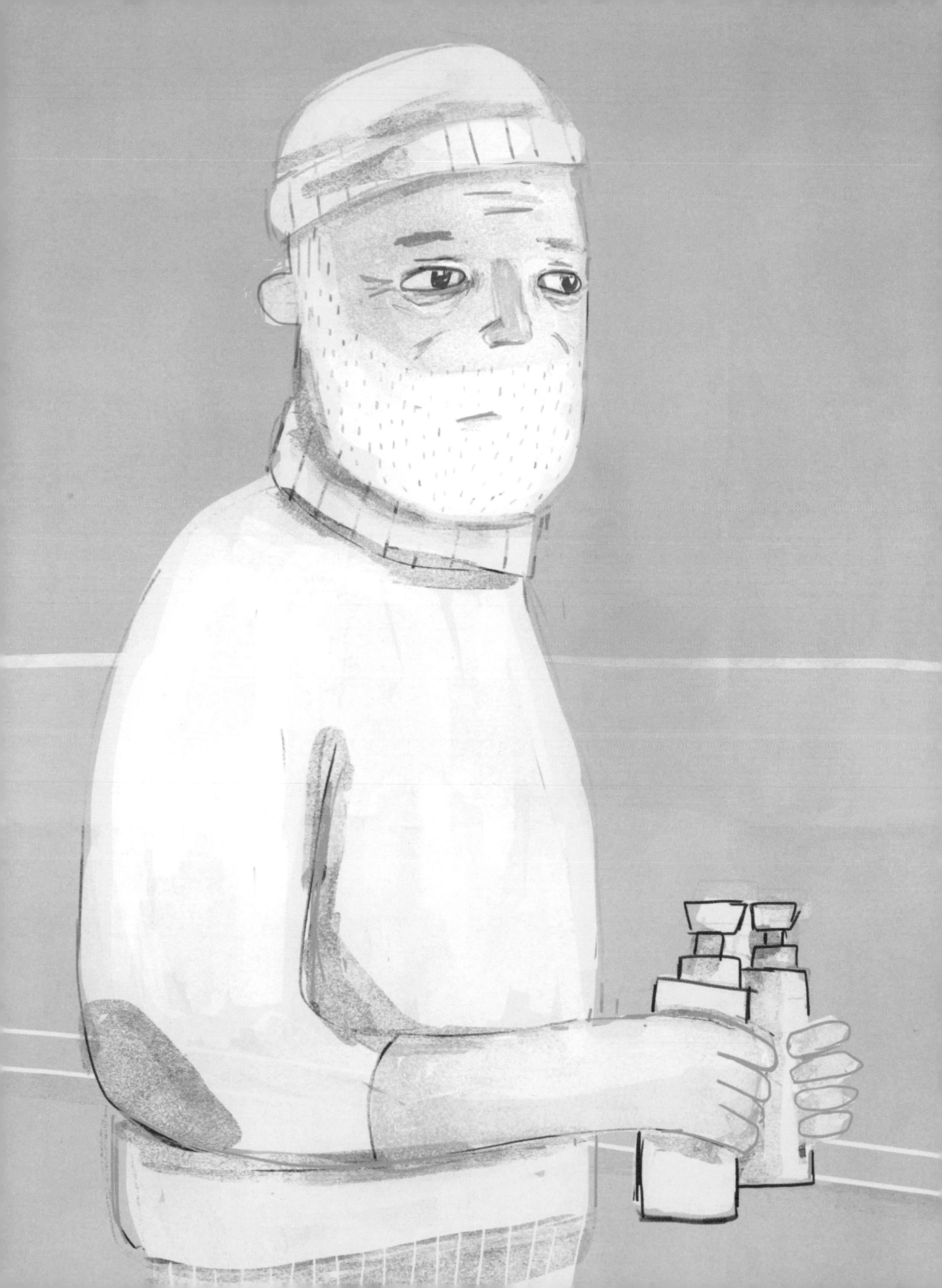

So much hate and rancor
and emptiness

for just one
heart.

It would have broken
anyone else.

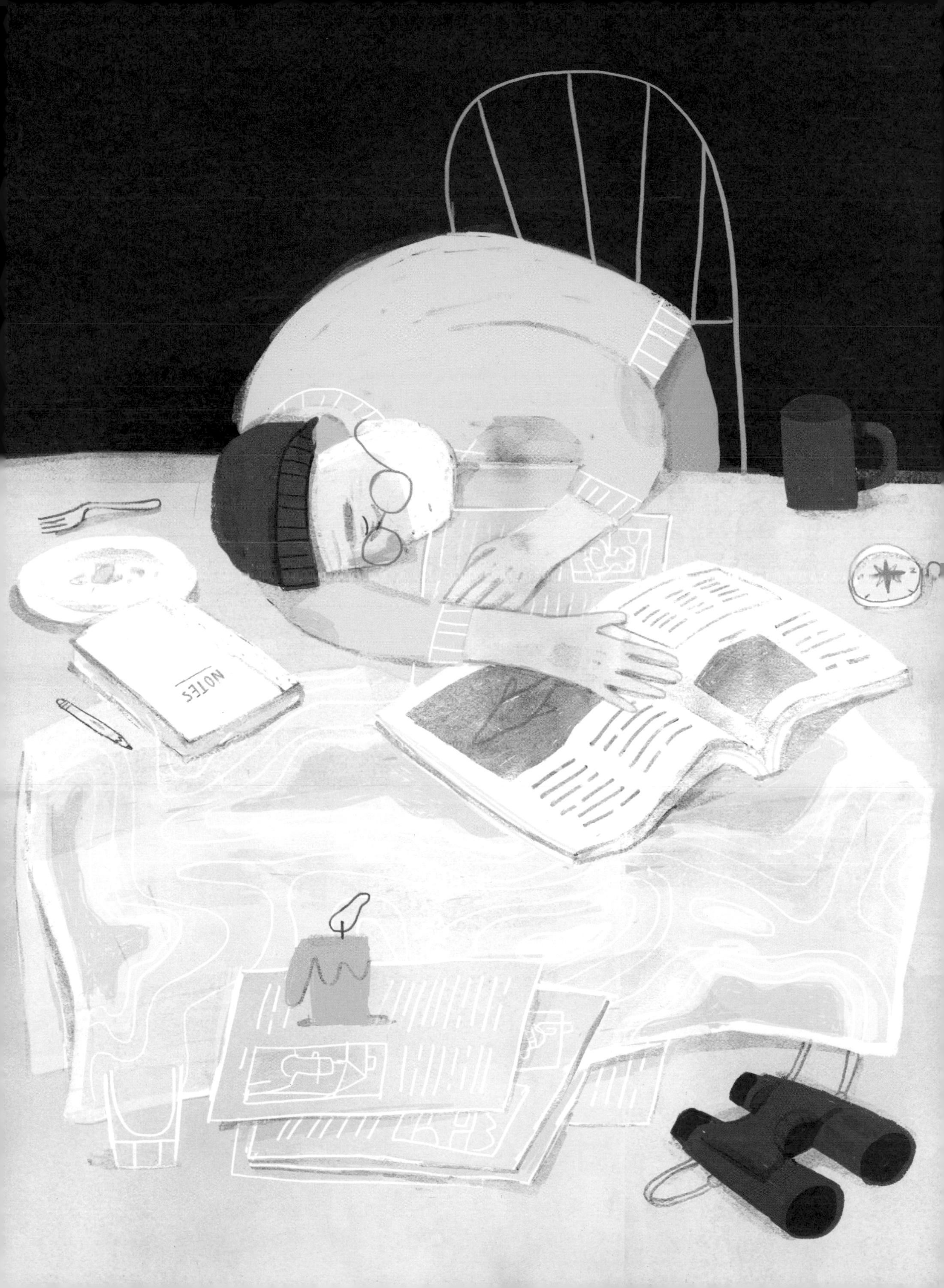
NOTES

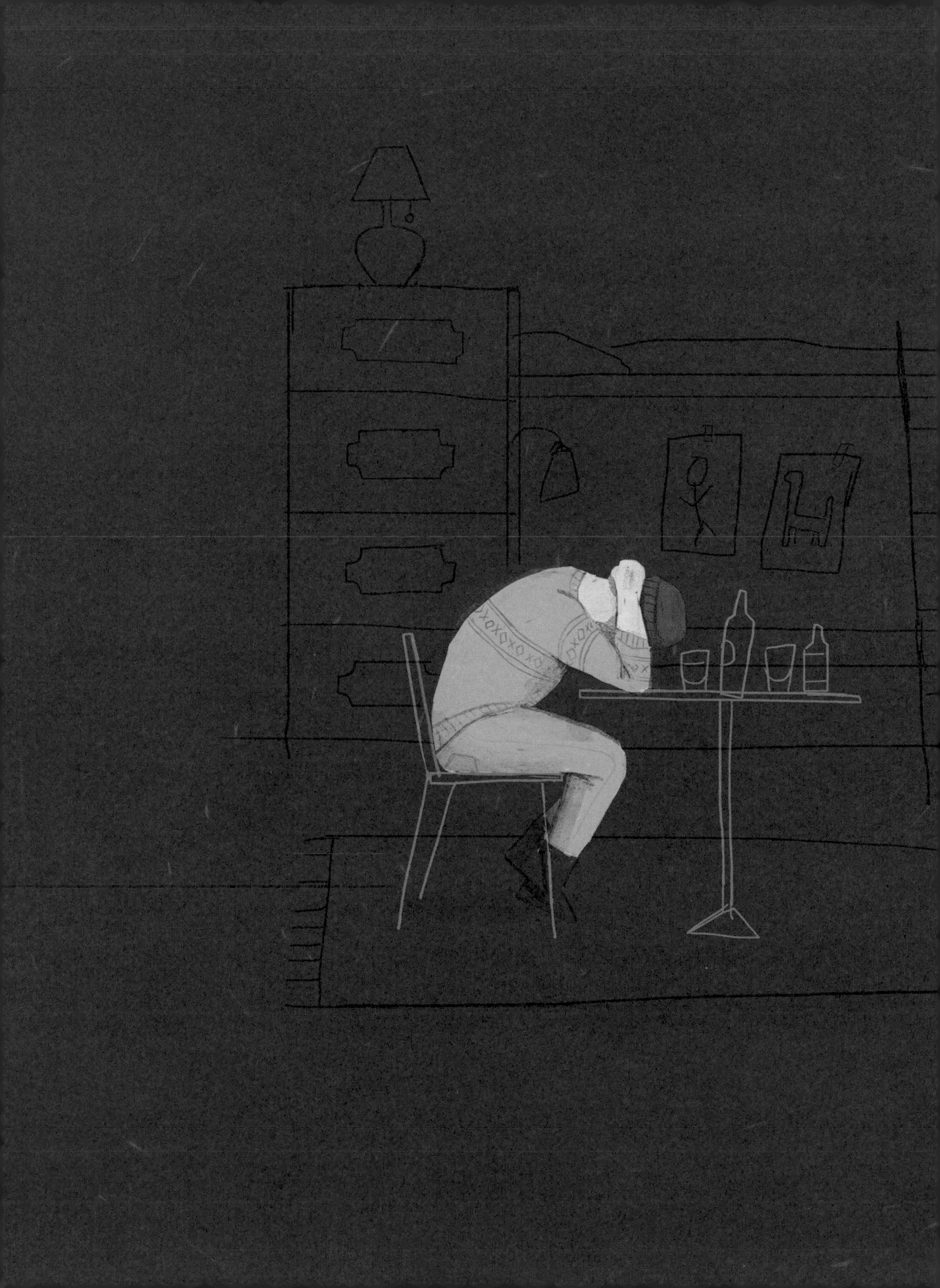

But not Jack,
who decided to
change.

Jack changed,
as the
summers,
springs,
falls,
and of course winters
made him into

another Jack.

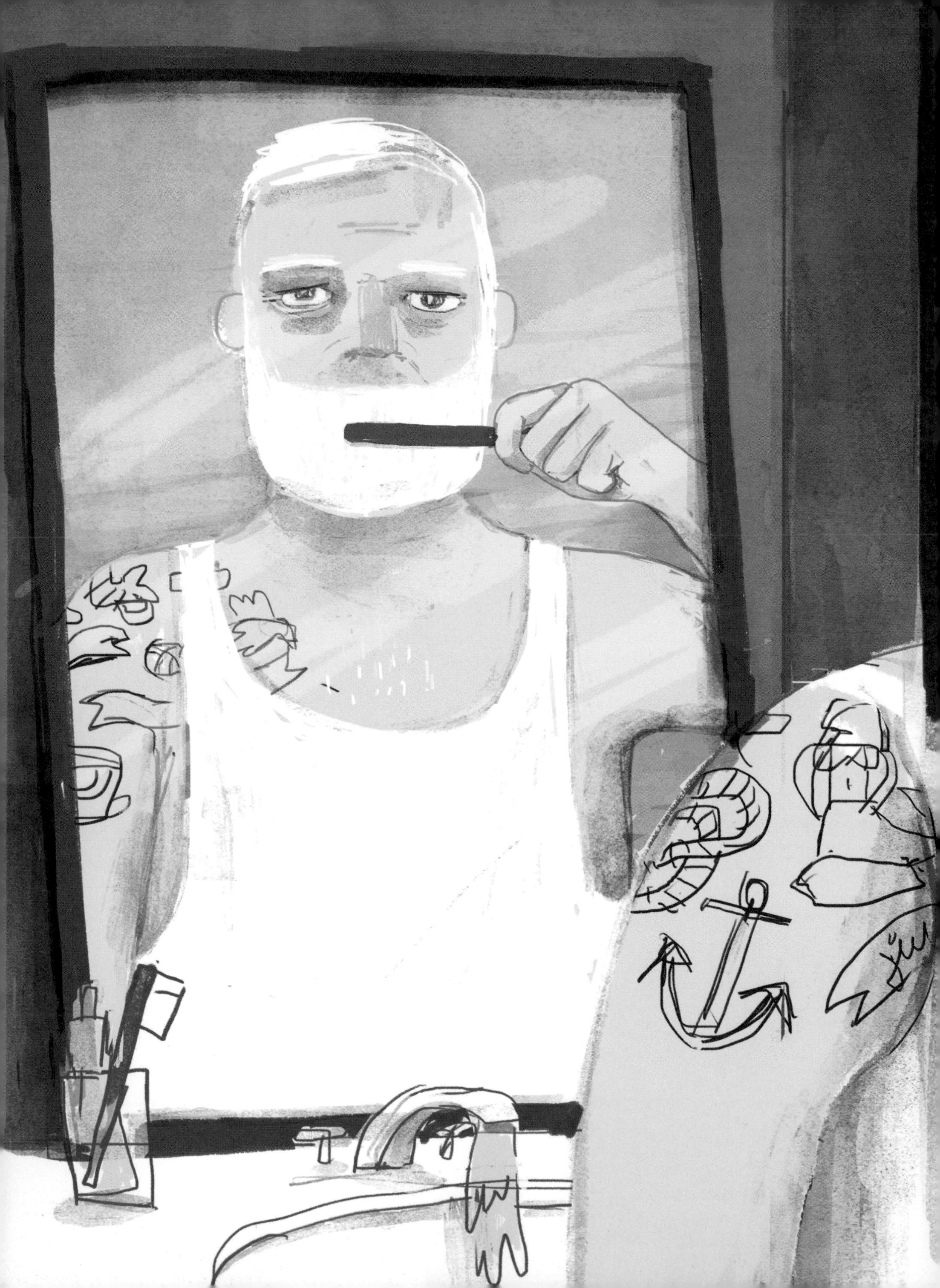

Gray,
mean,
dark,

and ugly.

Unrecognizable.

And then,
on a night not much different
from other nights,

he saw it
lurking
around his boat.

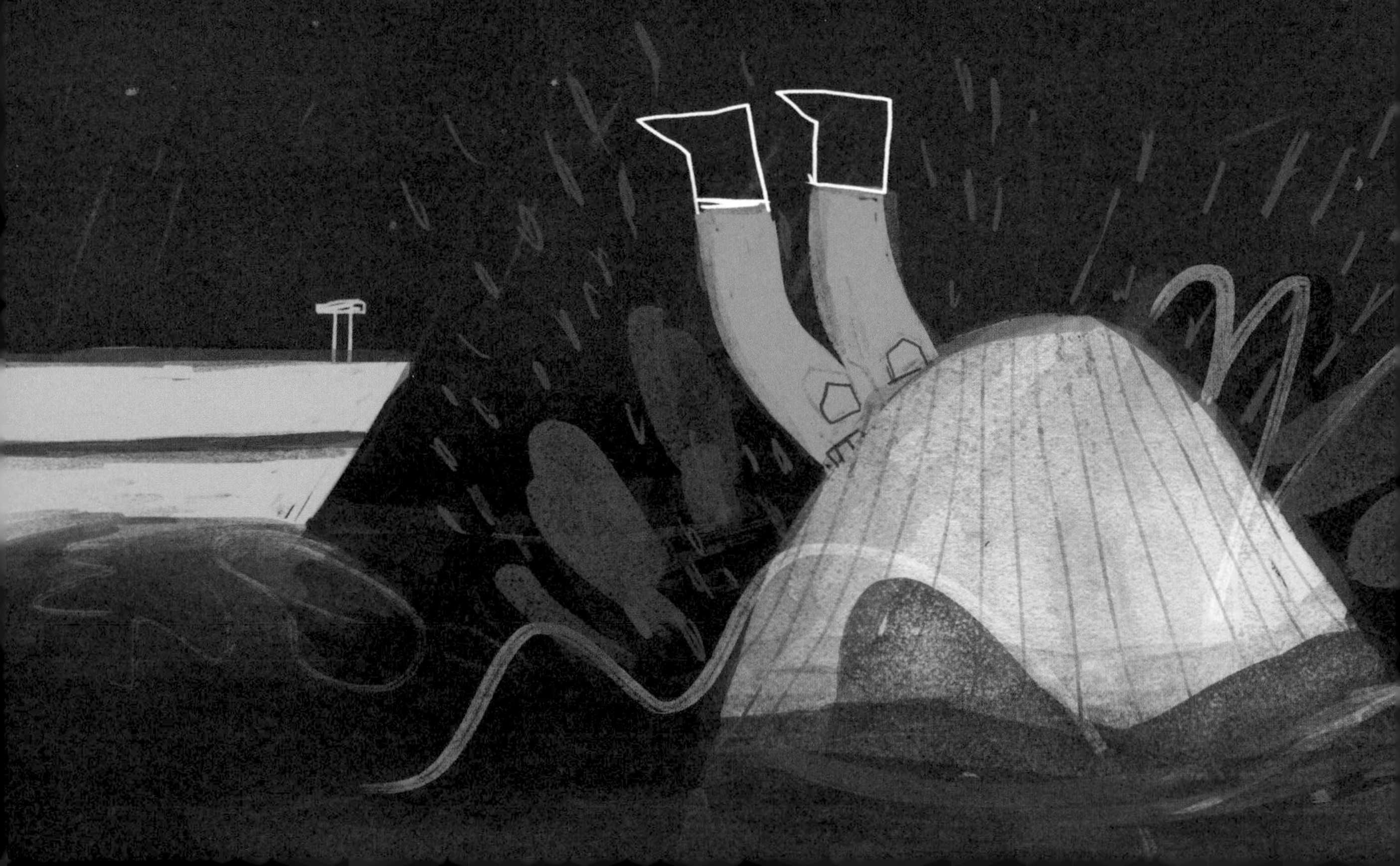

The whale. Yes,
the gray one with the scarred
dorsal fin.

Needless to say, Jack didn't waste a moment
before throwing himself into the mouth of the beast

with such force that he ended up—
poof—
deep in the whale's belly.

The belly of the beast he had been
looking for.

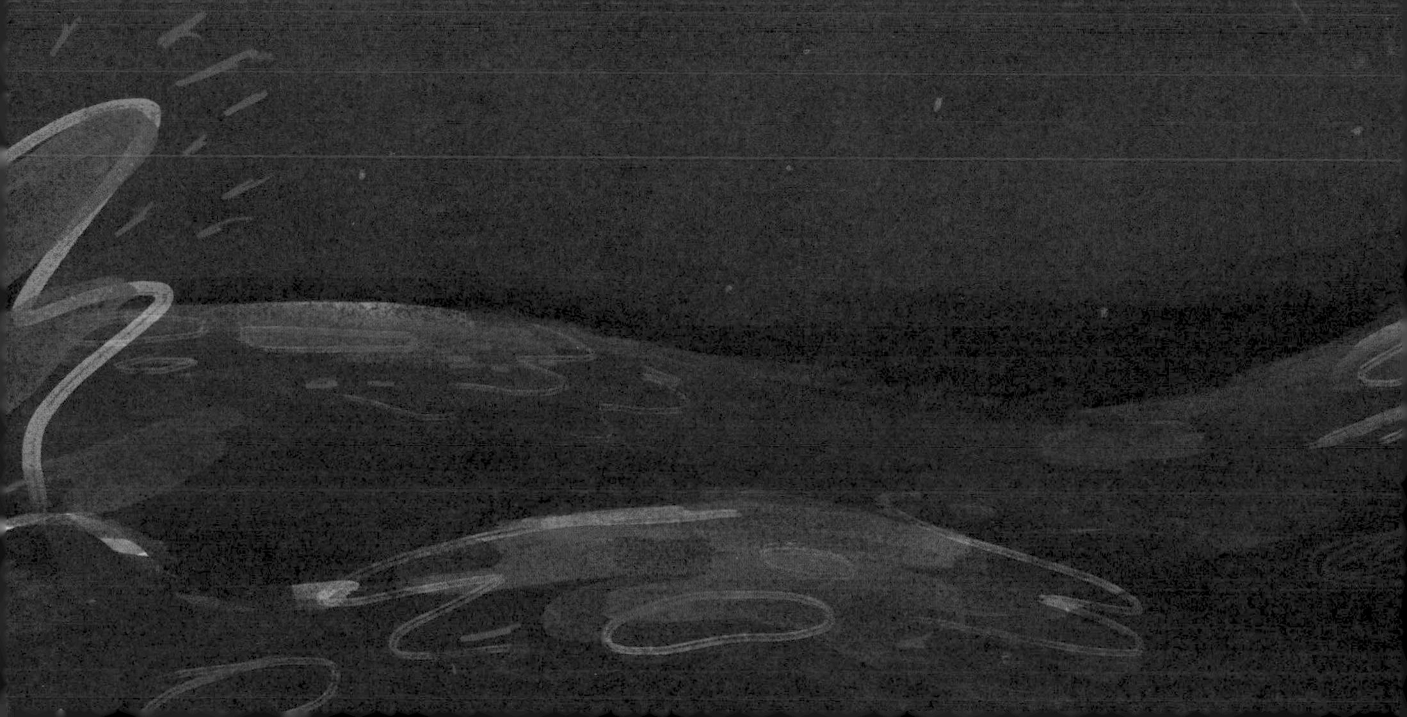

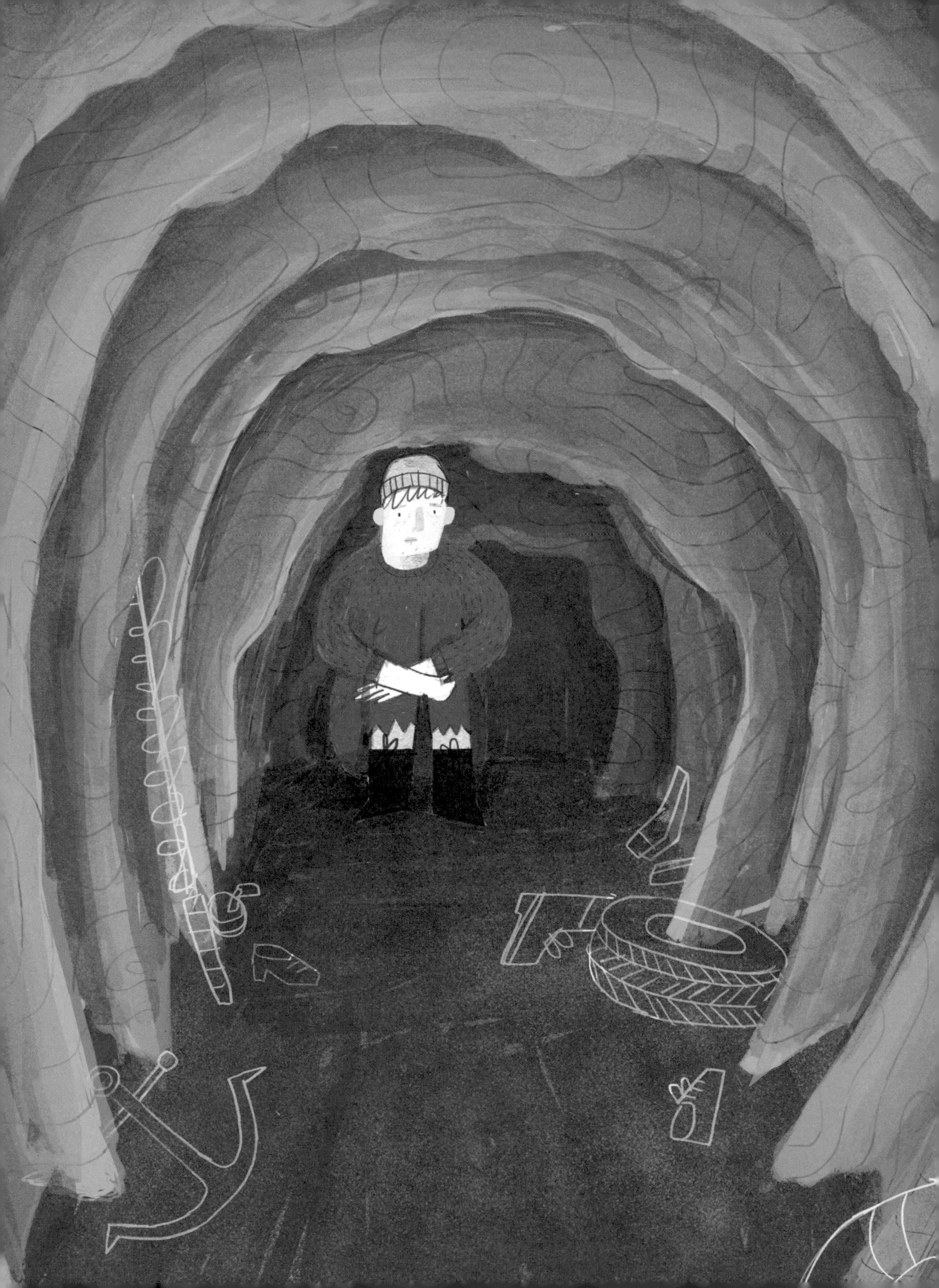

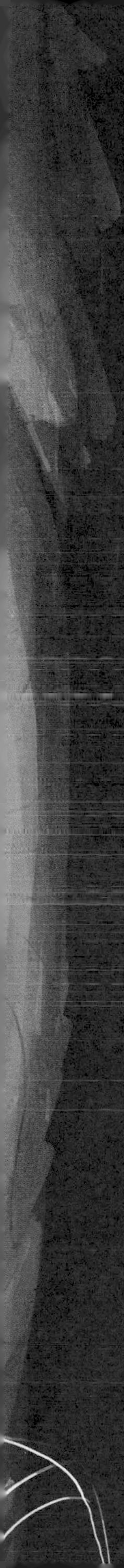

When he got to the bottom,
Jack
sat up
and saw that Julos was there.

Dirty, sad, and all alone
but very much
alive.

"Who are you and what are you doing here?"
"I'm your father! It's me, Jack!"

Julos got up, came over,
and ran his fingers
over each feature
of Jack's face.

"Impossible. My father doesn't have your eyes,
your sad eyes, or your frown.
My father is...a good man.
Leave, please!"

With no time to say yes or no
or do
anything,

Jack realized he had just been banished
from the belly of the whale.

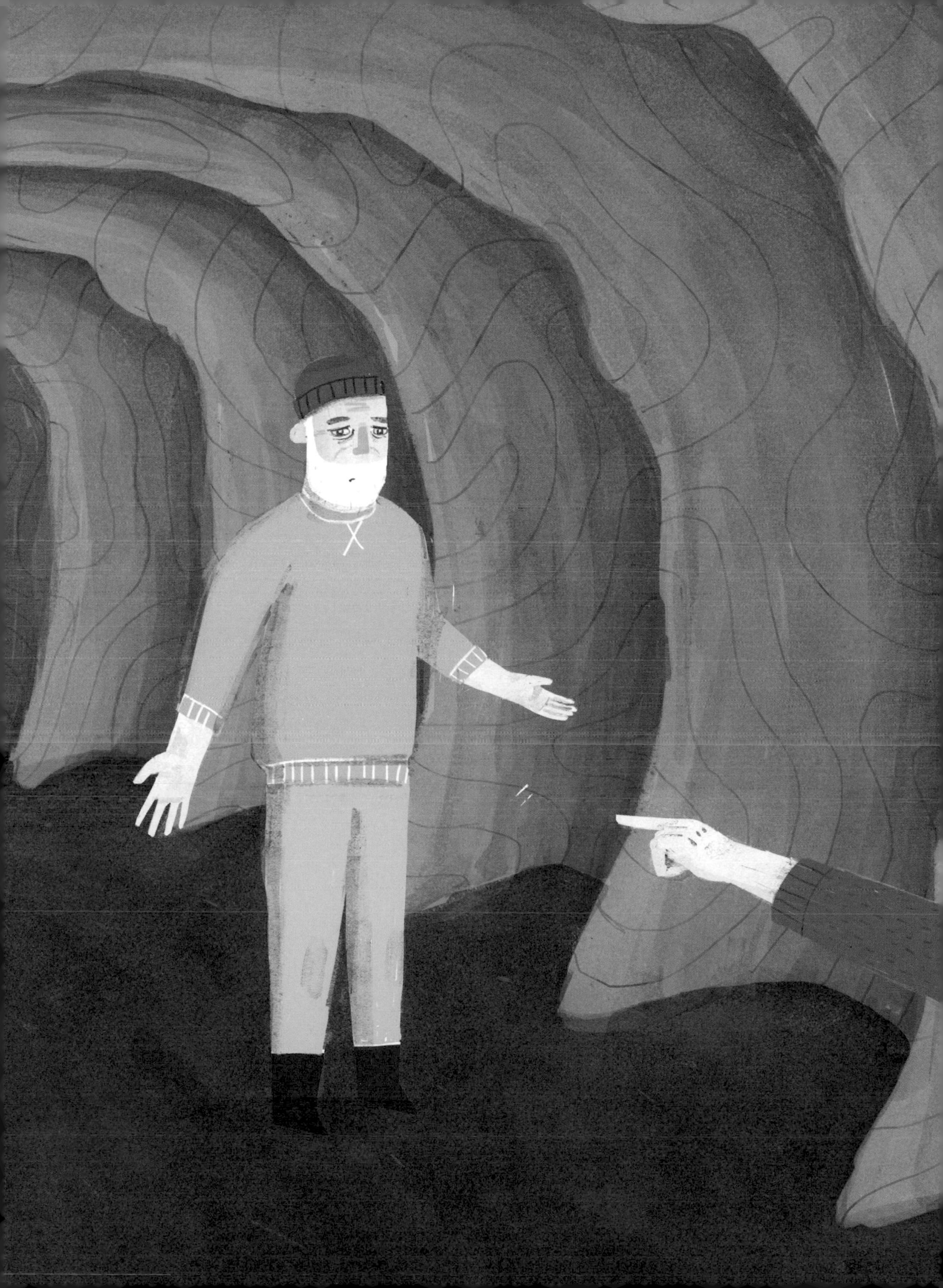

Yet
he didn't

move.

Jack ran his fingers
over each feature
of his own face.

"Whose face is this?"
"Why, it's yours, sir."
"And this rough, hardened skin,
whose skin is this?"
"Why, it's yours, sir."

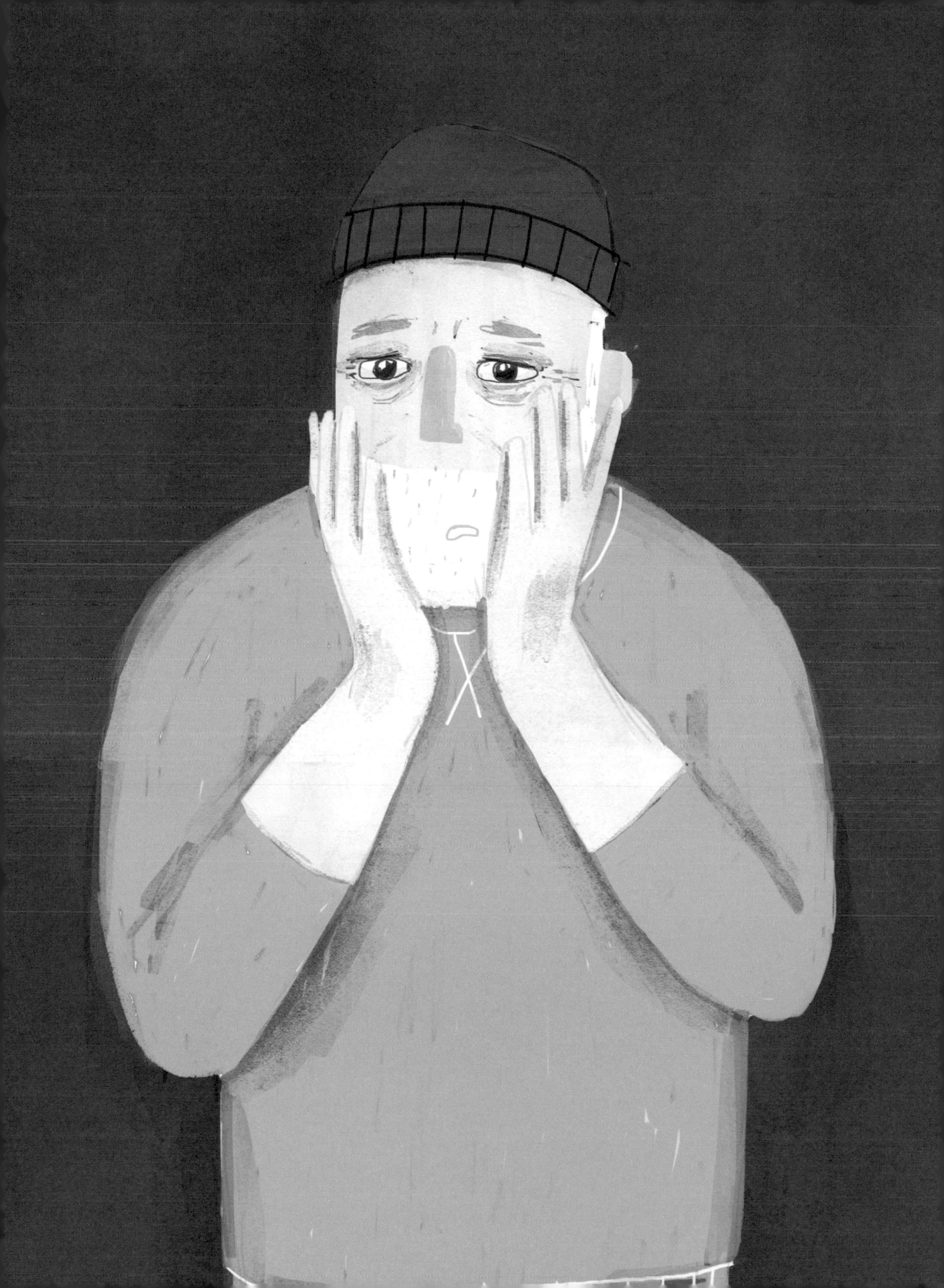

Jack stood up,
took a step back,
and another,
and another.

If Jack could have gone far away and never returned
he would have.

But it's impossible to leave the belly of a whale
like that—
poof.

So Jack just walked away,
leaving nothing
behind him

but a trail
of unbearable pain,

and
the clatter
of a despairing heart.

Just then

(for some reason)
Julos shouted.

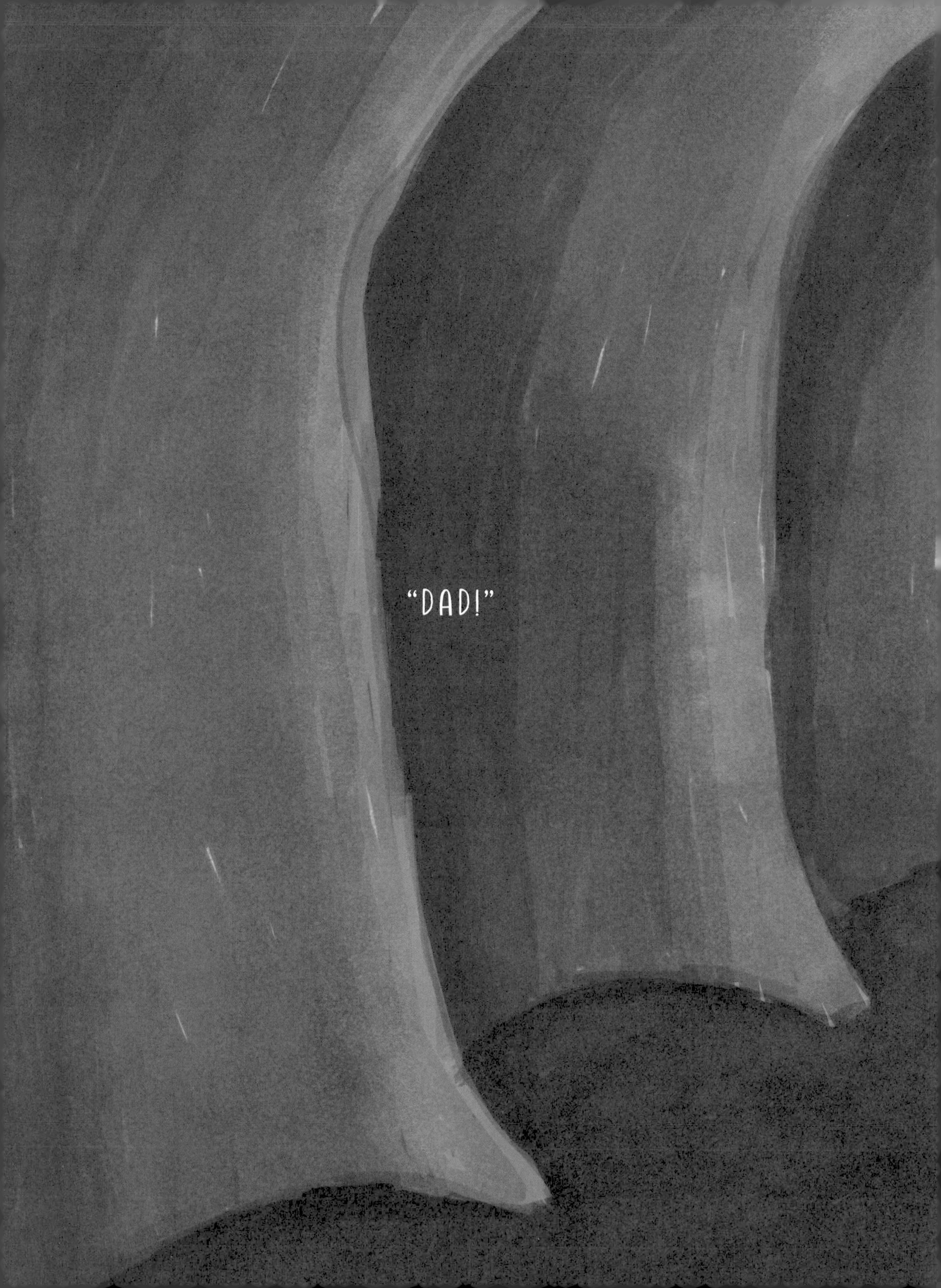
"DAD!"

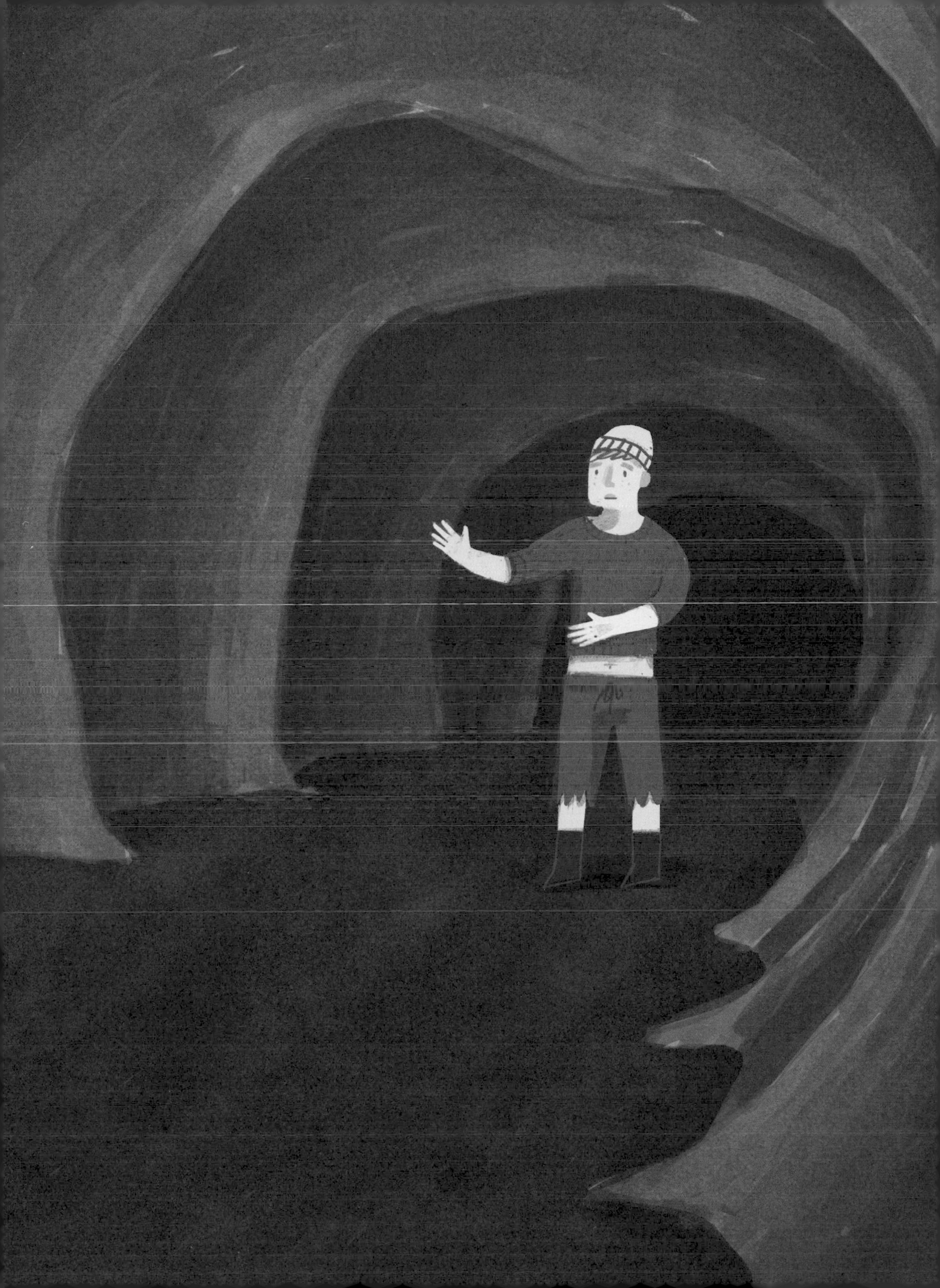

Nobody knows
how
or when
Jack and Julos managed
to climb out

from the whale's insides.

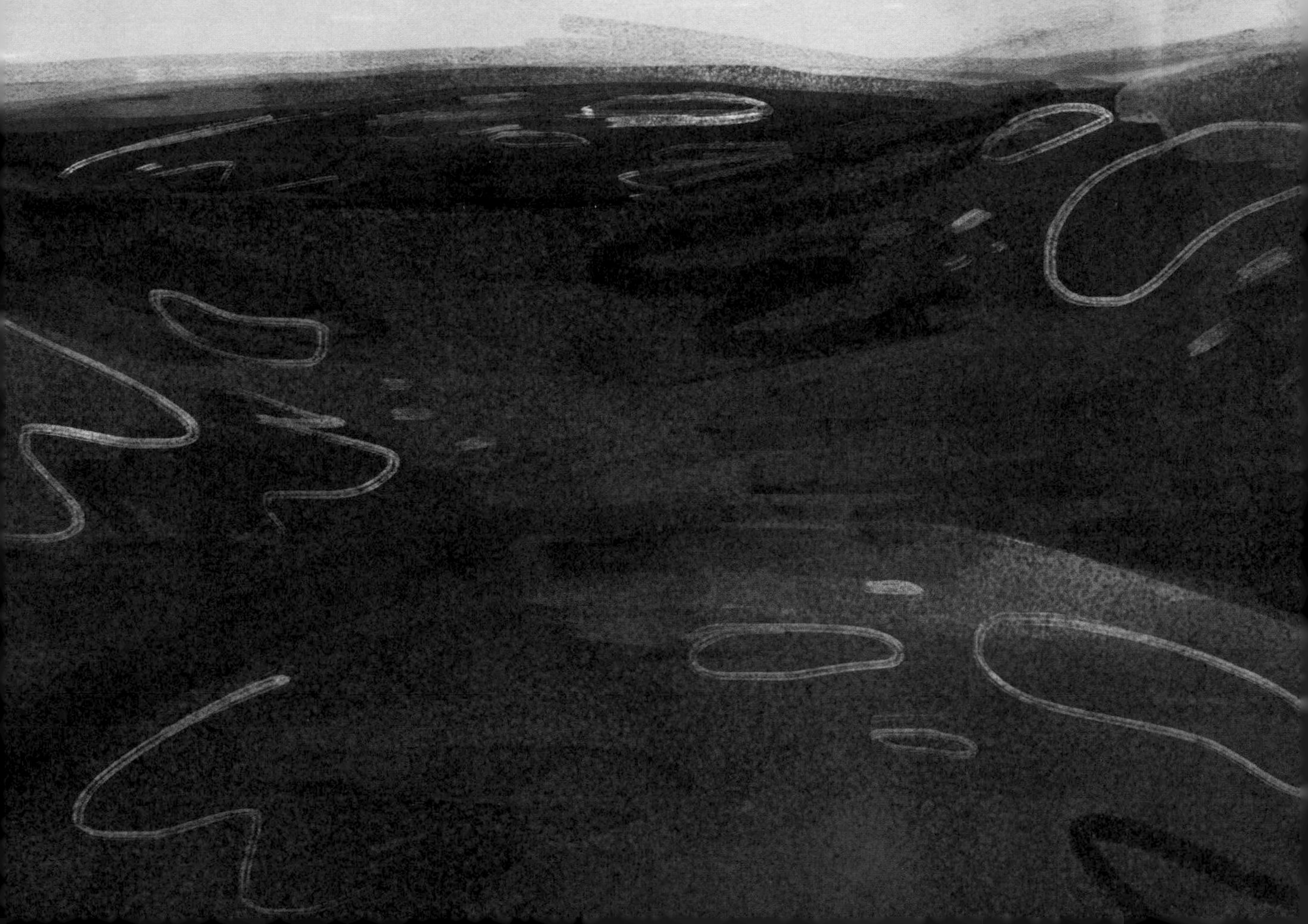

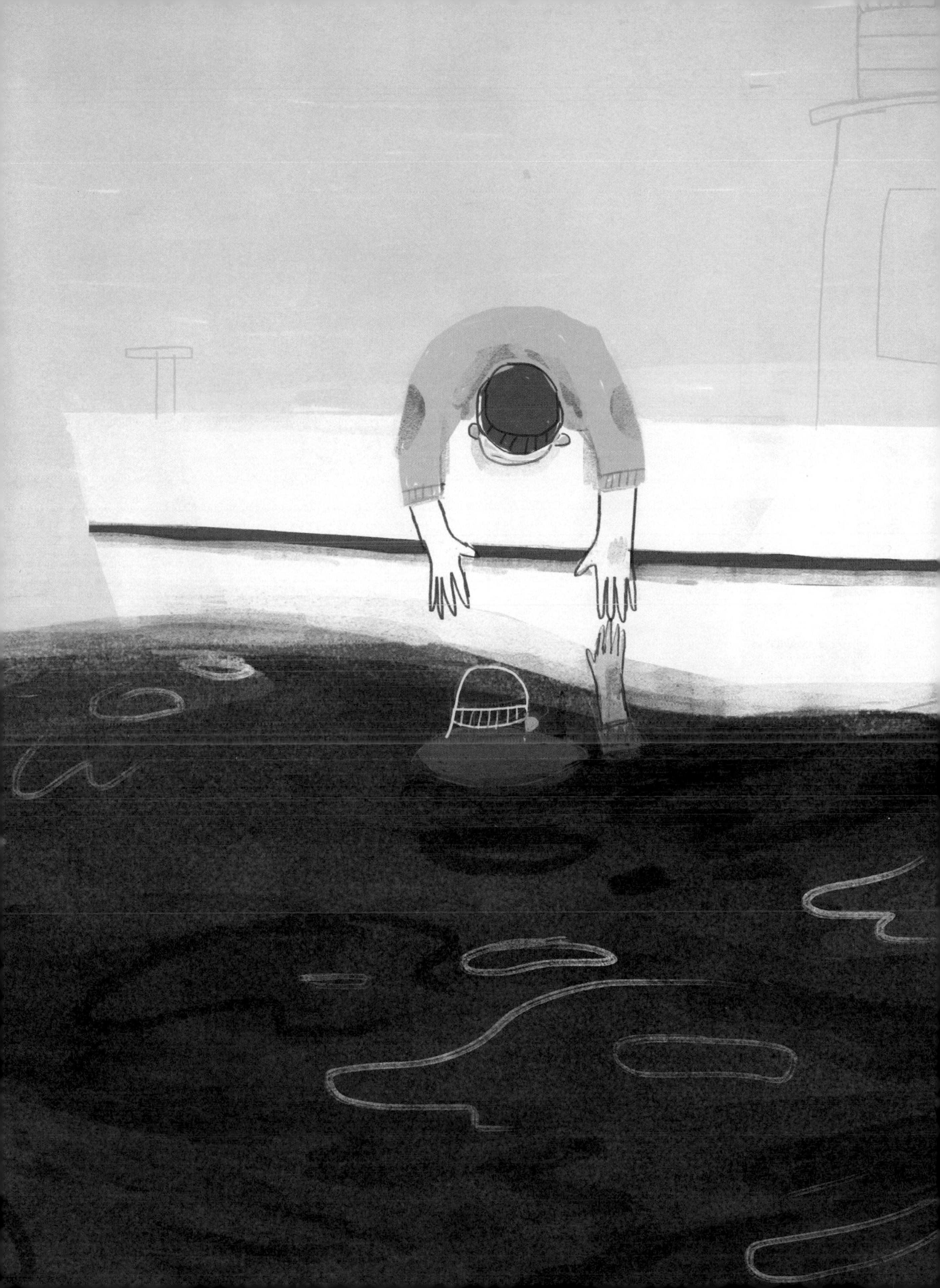

But one thing is certain:
Jack had lost too much
time.

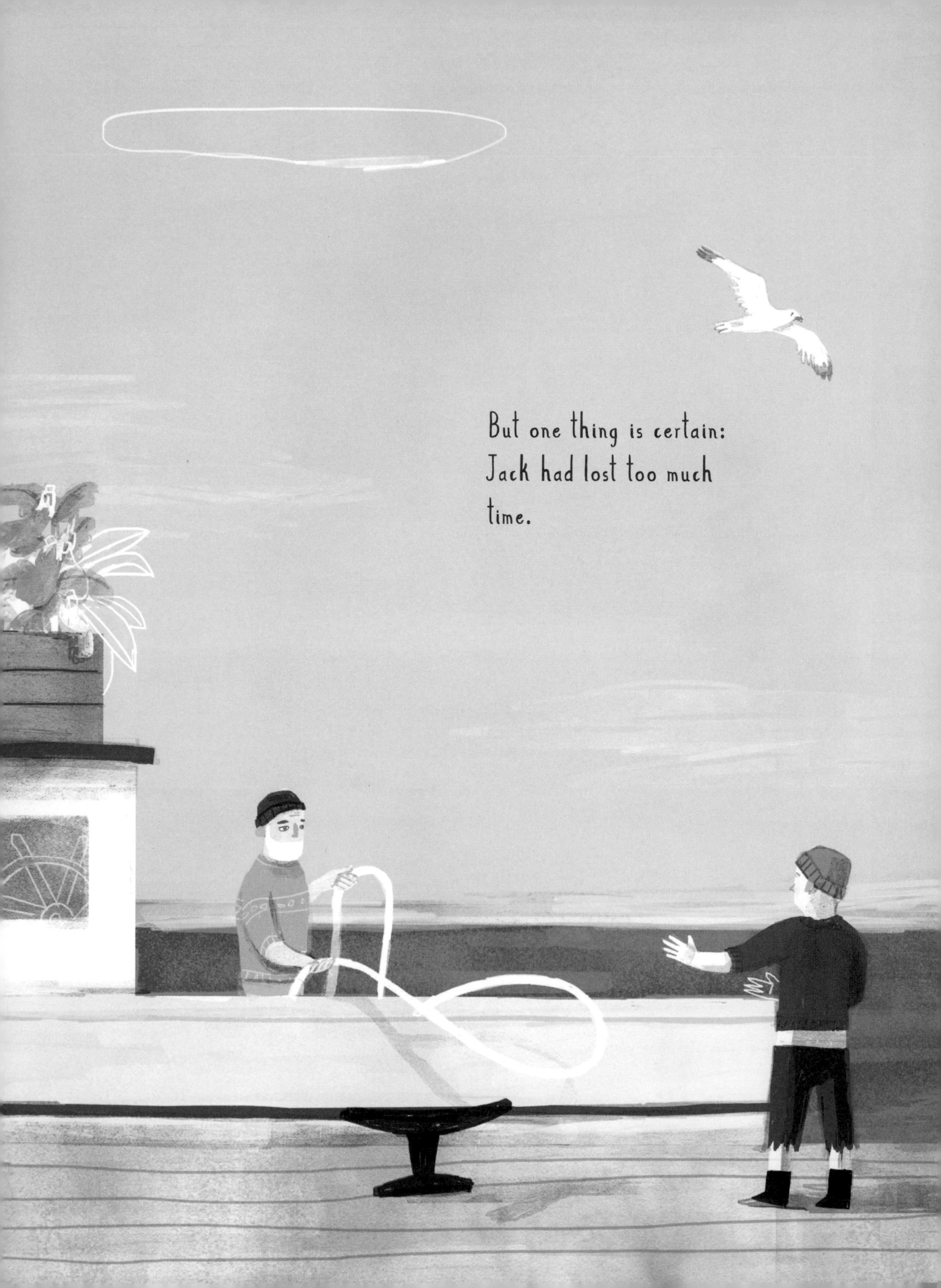

And nothing
would ever be
like it was before.

He realized this
once he docked his boat
and asked everyone he met
along the way

where the woman
he loved
had gone.

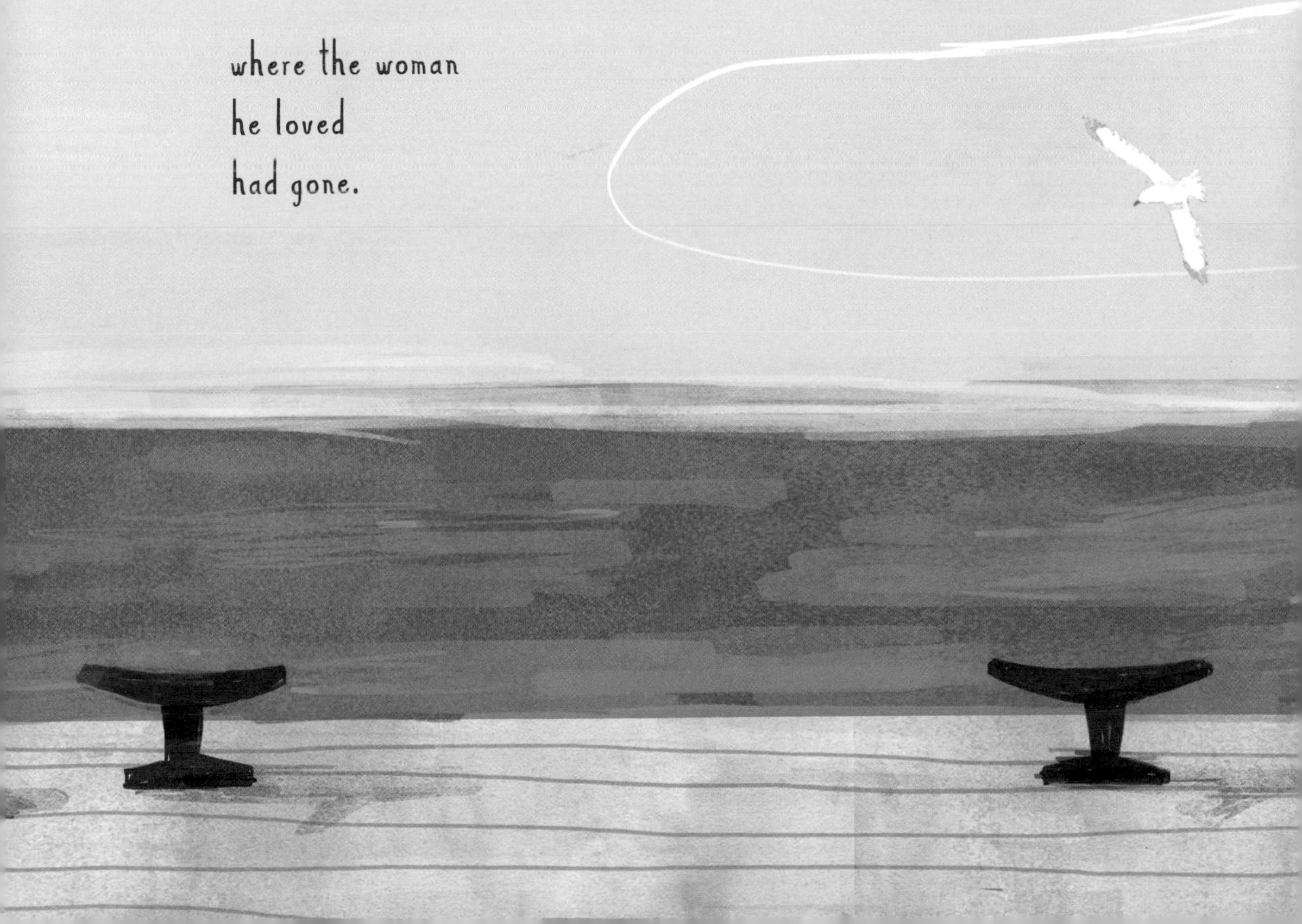

They all said
exactly the same
thing

with exactly the same
hollow
eyes

and exactly the same
gray
words.

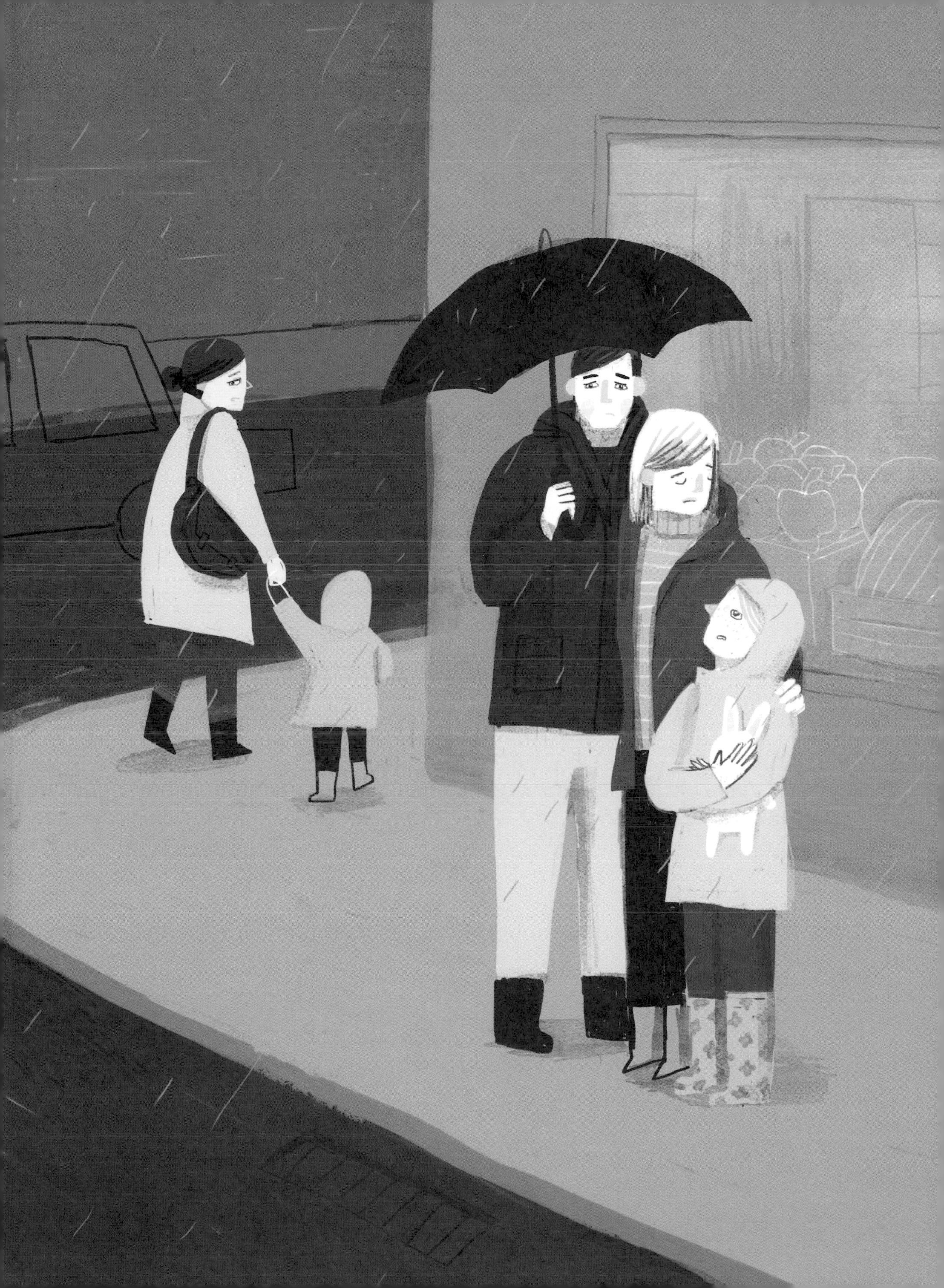

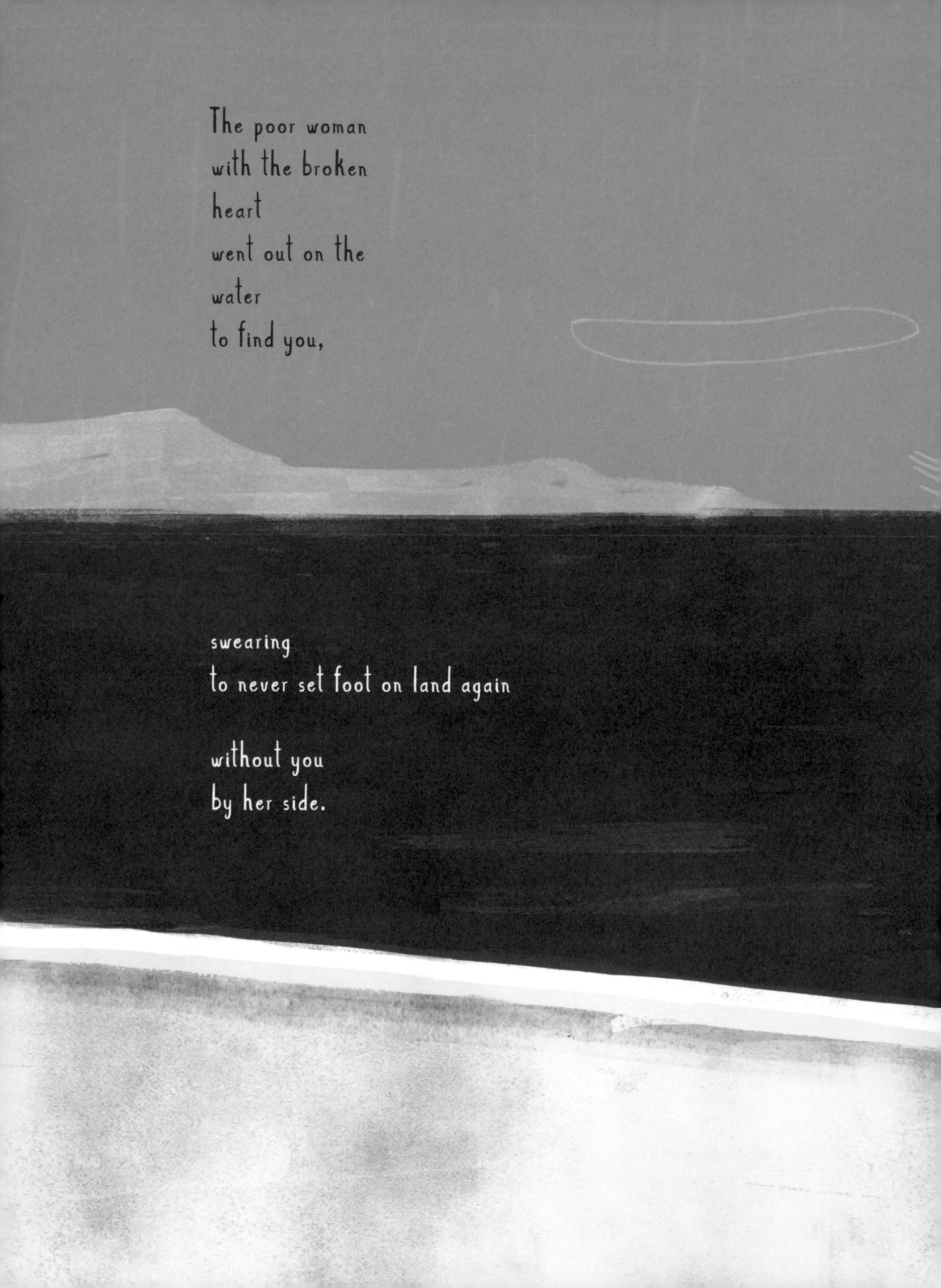

The poor woman
with the broken
heart
went out on the
water
to find you,

swearing
to never set foot on land again

without you
by her side.

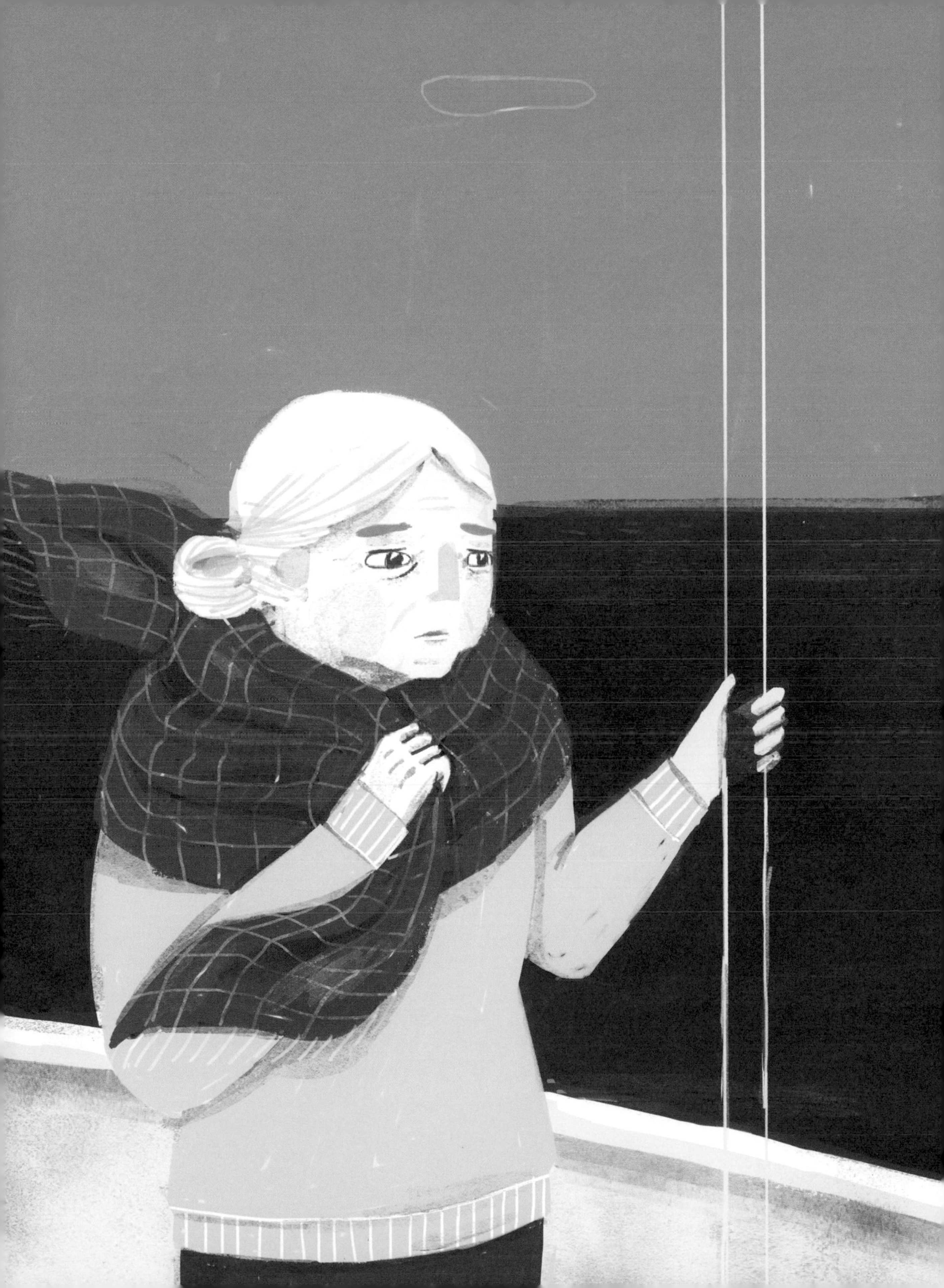

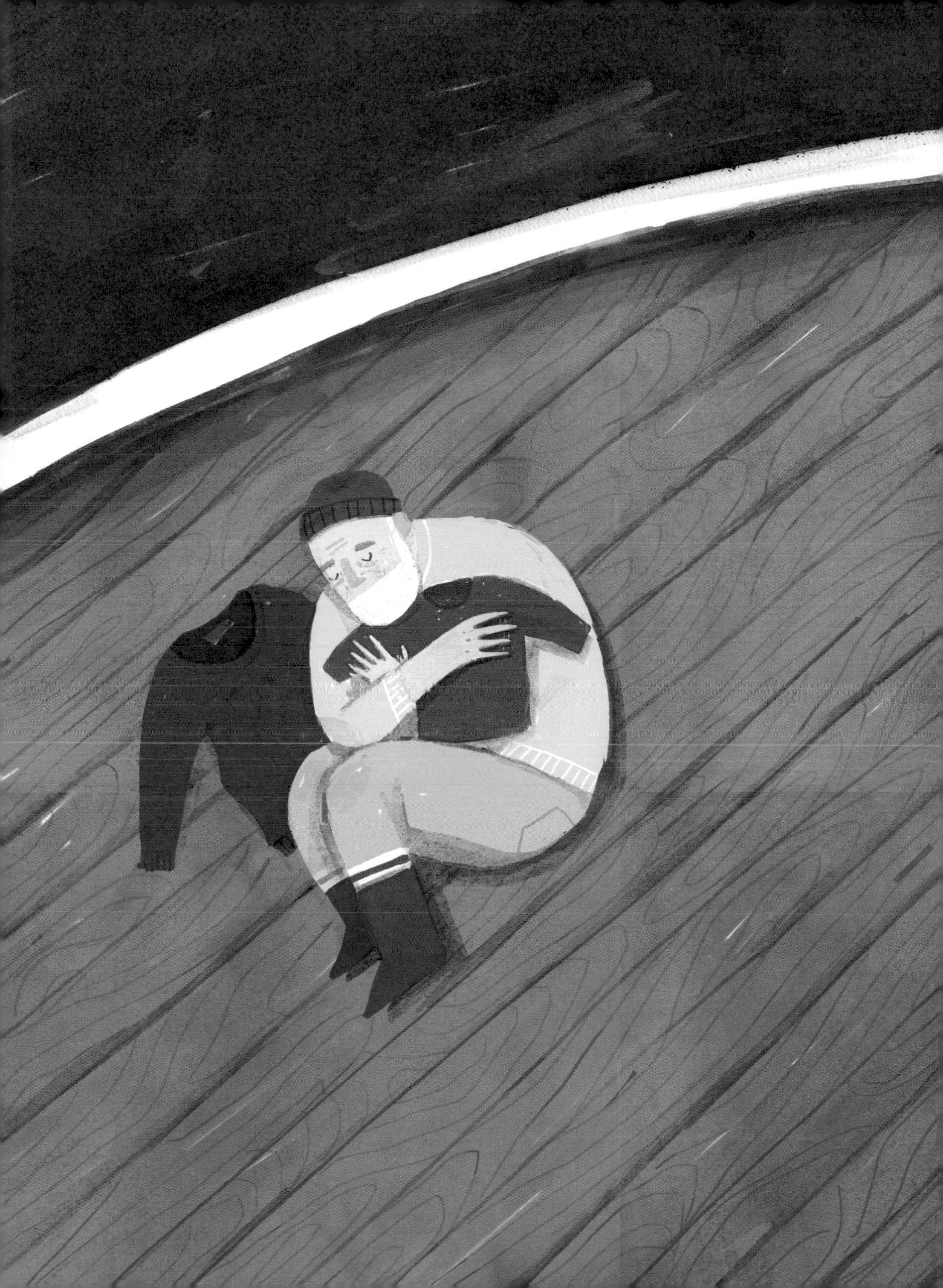